T0361773

Virginie Grimaldi was born in 1977 in Bordeaux, where she still lives. She is the author of nine novels and was the most read French writer for three consecutive years (in 2019, 2020, and 2021). Her novels have been bestsellers in Europe and have been translated into more than twenty languages.

For Europa Editions, **Hildegarde Serle** has translated the bestselling *Mirror Visitor* series by Christelle Dabos and Valérie Perrin's bestselling *Fresh Water for Flowers*. She lives in London.

Dear reader,

I'm entrusting Emma and
Agathe to you, over one summer
in the Basque Country.
I wish you a
good read (and a good life).

Yours,
Virginie Grimaldi

A GOOD LIFE

Virginie Grimaldi

A GOOD LIFE

Translated from the French
by Hildegarde Serle

Europa
editions

Europa Editions
27 Union Square West, Suite 302
New York NY 10003
www.europaeditions.com
info@europaeditions.com

This book is a work of fiction. Any references to historical events,
real people, or real locales are used fictitiously.

Copyright © Flammarion, 2023
First publication 2024 by Europa Editions
This edition, 2025 by Europa Editions

Translation by Hildegarde Serle
Original title: *Une belle vie*
Translation copyright 2024 by Europa Editions

All rights reserved, including the right of reproduction
in whole or in part in any form.

Library of Congress Cataloging in Publication Data is available
ISBN 979-8-88966-105-4

Grimaldi, Virginie
A Good Life

Cover illustration and design by Ginevra Rapisardi

Prepress by Grafica Punto Print – Rome

Printed in the USA

"It's like an invisible chain
Had linked our wrists
On the day we were born
So if you sink, I sink, too
And I'm far too fond of life
For that to be allowed."
—CLARA LUCIANI, "My Sister"

For my sister.

A GOOD LIFE

My sister was born this morning. She's ugly.
She's all red and all streaky.
Daddy asks if I'm pleased, I say no. I'm not pleased. I don't want her. I hope they're going to leave her at the hospital.
I won't lend her my toys.
But I do like her teddy.

TODAY
AUGUST 5
EMMA

2:32 P.M.

The gate's not bolted. It creaks as I push it open, as if reproaching me for not having come for a long time. The white paint has flaked off in places, revealing the original black. After Mima was burgled, I insisted she get an alarm installed, as well as a padlock and several motion-sensor spotlights around the house. She tried every excuse: "The cat will set off the alarm;" "I won't be able to open my windows;" "Monsieur Malois was burgled and the alarm didn't work;" "It's too expensive;" "Anyway, I've nothing worth stealing;" "Leave me in peace, Emma, you're as obstinate as your father."

I'm the first to arrive. The shutters are closed, weeds have crept up between the flagstones of the terrace, the tomato plants are weighed down with fruit. Mima planted them on my birthday. She phoned me just after, cursing the soil lodged under her nails that refused to wash away. "I planted some beefsteak tomatoes, I know you like them," she told me. "I'll make you a fine salad when you come."

Right beside the beefsteaks, there's a cherry-tomato plant, Agathe's favorite. I pick one, wipe it on my shirt, and sink my teeth into it. The skin breaks, the flesh bursts out and spills over my lips, the sharp juice leaving seeds on my tongue, and it's childhood memories that come knocking.

"You're already here?"

Agathe's voice makes me jump. I didn't hear her arrive. She clasps me in her arms, while mine remain dangling. In the family, we're pretty stingy with displays of affection. But not my sister. She's fluent in hugging and wears her heart on her sleeve.

"I'm happy to see you!" she says, relaxing her grip. "After all this time . . . "

She breaks off, stares at me, and I get emotional when her eyes meet mine.

"I was amazed when I got your message," she continues. "Great idea you had. I'm livid about Mima's house being sold, but it's no surprise coming from our dear uncle. The guy's still asking me for the twenty centimes he lent me when I was eight, I'm sure he was a parking meter in another life."

"It would explain his square head."

"Yeah. If you press on his nose, he shits a parking ticket. Right, shall we open up the house?"

I follow her to the door. Sunlight splashes her hair, and some long white strands show up in her blond mop. My heart contracts at this evidence of time passing. When I saw her every day, my little sister didn't age. We're five years older since the last time, and suddenly Agathe has become an adult.

"Don't know where I shoved the key."

She empties her bag out onto the doormat, the long bronze key lies there, in the middle of the packs of chewing gum and cigarettes.

"There it is!"

I'd have liked it not to be there. For us to leave, unable to enter, forced to give up. I'd have liked never to have suggested to my sister that we come to spend our last vacation here, like when we were little, before the house belongs to others. I'd have liked never to know the feeling of this door opening without our grandmother's voice asking us to take off our shoes.

A gathe's pooped in the bath again. Her turds are bobbing all around me. Mommy takes her out of the water, shrieking. She often shrieks, since Agathe.

When Daddy gets home from work, Mommy tells him. He laughs, so she laughs, too. I give them a cuddle.

Tomorrow, I'm starting at primary school. I hope I'll be in Cécile's class, but not in Margaux's. She shows off too much about her long hair, and also, she told me I was dumb because I couldn't ride a bike without stabilizers.

I want long hair, too, but Mommy won't let me. She says it's too much of a pain to wash because of my curls. She cuts it short with the big orange scissors. When I'm big, I'll have long hair like Margaux.

2:35 P.M.

Before I've even set foot in the house, the alarm starts wailing. At least it puts paid to any tears. Emma jumps like popcorn, before sticking her fingers in her ears. Note for later: if I plan on doing a burglary, don't ask my sister to join me.

I tap out the code on the keypad. Mima had shared it with me when she was in hospital, so I could come and feed the cat.

8085.

The years her two granddaughters were born.

I open the downstairs shutters, Emma deals with those upstairs. I join her in Mima's bedroom, and find her rooted to the spot in front of the chest of drawers. The jewelry box lies open, empty. She shakes her head:

"Clearly, the parking meter remembered he had a mother."

"I'd pay a lot to see his face when he discovers that most of the jewelry's fake."

"Does he know we're here?"

"No. I've not spoken to him since the funeral."

Silence descends. I said the taboo word. Emma didn't come to Mima's funeral. Supposedly, a school trip she couldn't cancel. Can't imagine a destination that could take priority over saying farewell to our grandmother, but I wasn't in a position to interfere.

We go back down to the sitting room. On the waxed cloth over the little wooden table, the TV program lies open at Friday May 27. In the basket, the apples are shriveled.

"Take the cheese and fruit home with you," Mima told me, on

one of my hospital visits. "I could be here for a while, they'll go off."

I refused to do so, out of superstition. She was recovering a little each day, the doctors were confident.

"I'm not going to eat your rotten cheese," I said. "An entire town could be wiped out just by opening your fridge. Don't know why they bother to build nuclear bombs when there's camembert."

She laughed, so I went on:

"Why d'you think you've lost all your teeth? It's not age, Mima, it's the stink."

The nurse's aide brought in supper, Mima smiled on seeing the slice of bland cheese wrapped in cellophane. I kissed her forehead and promised I'd be back tomorrow. At 4:56 in the morning, a stroke more severe than the previous one took away all our tomorrows.

Emma opens the fridge:

"We need to go shopping."

"We can do it tomorrow, no? I'd rather go to the beach. The weather's fantastic, let's make the most of it, never lasts long here."

She doesn't need to insist, her eyes give me the message. She sits at the table and starts writing a list. The honeymoon has lasted barely a few minutes, and it's back to the old routine, as if we'd left it behind just yesterday.

"What d'you have for breakfast?"

"Coffee," I reply, trying to hide my disappointment.

She writes it down. Her hair's very short, in profile she could be our mother. I'd never noticed how like her she is. Apparently, I got my looks entirely from my father, particularly his nose. Not sure I'm grateful for that, even considered having it surgically tweaked, but in the end, I kept it as it is—could come in handy. If I'm on a boat one day and the tiller stops working, for example.

"We could have veal tonight?" Emma suggests.

"I'm vegetarian."

"Since when?"

"Two or three years."

"Right. You do eat chicken, though?"

"No, but you can get some for yourself."

"Oh, no, never mind. We'll eat fish."

"I don't eat seafood either."

"But what do you feed yourself on? Seeds?"

"Only seeds, yes. In fact, I'll have to watch out because I've noticed something weird. Look."

I move closer to her and lift up the sleeve of my T-shirt.

"Can't see anything," she says.

"Yes, there, look closer. You can't see it?"

"No."

"I'm starting to sprout feathers. And the other day, I laid an egg."

She rolls her eyes and returns to her list, but I can clearly see her mouth struggling not to laugh.

YESTERDAY
NOVEMBER 1986
AGATHE—1½ YEARS OLD

No.

3:10 P.M.

The supermarket is almost deserted. Just a few older folks have come to enjoy the cool of the frozen-food aisle. Everyone's at the beach. I can picture the serried ranks of towels, the kids' feet sending sand flying into eyes, the calls of concerned parents, the laughter of others, the exhausting heat. I no longer find any charm in those waves I spent my childhood in, or the hot sand trampled in adolescence. I used to count the days keeping me from the ocean, which always seemed more beautiful than when last I'd left it, but I can now envisage the rest of my life without it. I don't hate it, it's worse: it's become dispensable.

"I'm going to look for the TP," Agathe announces, moving off.

I cross toilet paper off the list. I'd divided my list into aisles, dry goods first, then fresh produce, then, finally, frozen food.

My sister returns with her arms full of items, and none resemble toilet paper.

"I found brioche with chocolate chips! D'you remember Mima's?"

"Agathe, we wrote a list."

"*You* wrote a list," she retorts. "And *you* insisted that we plan for every meal of the week."

I don't respond. We've been together barely a few hours, and must remain so for seven days. There'll be no shortage of occasions for sparks to fly.

She opens the pack and tears off some brioche.

"Want some?"

She expects me to say no. I grab it and stuff it into my mouth. Don't want her, too, thinking I'm tight-assed.

It's Alex's favorite weapon, the reproach he pulls out when I go on about his lack of initiative: "You check everything after I've filled the dishwasher, you always find fault when I make a meal, you never approve of my suggestions for outings. Nothing I do is ever right, so I daren't do anything anymore."

Unanswerable. And, if I must be honest, not entirely wrong.

I've long loved his way of being in the world, of observing life with his quiet strength, his capacity for letting himself be carried along by it, adapting to whatever he found in it. He was the serenity I lacked; if I didn't feel it, I could live with it. I clung to him so he'd drag me away from childhood. I buried my anxieties inside his solid frame, his big arms totally enfolded me, I sheltered within them.

But time distorts other people's qualities and makes them seem like defects.

Agathe reseals the pack of brioche and throws me a cheeky smile:

"I'm off to find some chips, guess you didn't put them on your list."

I let her head off to the appropriate aisle, carefully avoiding warning her that she has a chocolate moustache.

We spent Christmas at Mima and Papi's. Uncle Jean-Yves and our cousins, Laurent and Jérôme, were all there. The four of us slept in the downstairs room, it was good fun, Agathe was snoring because she had a cold, sounded like Daddy's electric clippers. When we got up, we didn't even pee, just went straight to the tree to see if Father Christmas had left anything under it.

At school, Margaux told me he doesn't exist, I said he did, but the teacher said Margaux was right. I cried all through recess. In the evening, Daddy told me that was just nonsense, but then I didn't know who was telling the truth anymore, so I cried again. Daddy told me to stay in my room, that he'd prove to me that Father Christmas exists, but I must promise not to open the door. I promised, and wiped my nose on my sleeve.

Soon after, Daddy spoke to me through the door to my room. He was with Father Christmas, but I wasn't allowed to see him, I could only hear him. I got butterflies in my tummy. A booming voice said: "Ho, ho, ho, Emma, I am Father Christmas, I've come to tell you that I do exist, and will soon be coming to deliver presents for you and your little sister. Have you been a good girl this year?" I answered yes, even if I did steal a fry from Agathe's plate once. Apparently, he sees everything, but they were just too yummy.

He didn't stay long, but it doesn't matter, now I know he exists. I promised him I wouldn't tell anyone about it at school, but I still told Cécile, and Margaux a bit, and Olivier, Coumba, Natacha, and Vincent, because he's my boyfriend.

The presents were under the tree, but Papi and our parents were *still sleeping. Only Mima was awake, and we had to wait for the others to get up. She gave us hot milk and chocolate-chip brioche.*

I got a Popples cuddly toy, and best of all, a Speak & Spell. I played with it all day, so much that the batteries had to be changed! It proves that Father Christmas exists because it's exactly what I wrote in my letter that Mommy sent him. Margaux's a big fat liar.

Agathe got a Tiny Tears doll that pees (gross), and a firefly. It's like a cuddly toy, but its head lights up when she presses its tummy. Maybe we won't need to sleep with the corridor light on anymore, because I've had enough of it. I know that otherwise she gets anxious, but it stops me from sleeping, and I don't make a great fuss about that. She's sometimes cute, my sister, but all the same, it was easier before she turned up. I did write that in my letter to Father Christmas, too, but he obviously didn't understand the message.

YESTERDAY
DECEMBER 1987
AGATHE—2½ YEARS OLD

No *want bye-byes.*

4:01 P.M.

The heat charges into the mall as the automatic doors open. The cart is full, the items sorted by category into reusable bags. I suspect she considered doing so alphabetically.

"Now we've done your favorite activity, can we move on to mine?"

"Which one?"

"*La playa!*"

Emma rolls her eyes. She knows I won't give up, my special talent being getting what I want by wearing people down. That's how I got my job, how I got my apartment. And how I made Mathieu bolt, too. The jerk. When, for once, I was envisaging things being long-term, the guy cleared off before his trial period was over.

"Mind awfully giving me a hand?"

Emma has filled the car's trunk and it looks like a Tetris game. I grab the cart and head off to the storage area, wondering whether this week together was such a good idea after all.

I can't say I don't love my sister. She's even, undoubtedly, the person most at home in my heart since Mima left us in the lurch. But I'm convinced, because I feel it deeply, that one can both love someone and be unable to stomach them. Onions have the same effect on me.

I sometimes think that, if we weren't tied by blood, I wouldn't be able to put up with her. That all we share, these days, are our memories.

"Alright," she says, turning on the ignition. "As long as we go to the Chambre d'Amour beach."

I'd have preferred the Plage des Cavaliers, less known to

tourists, but whatever. A concession each, satisfaction for each. Emma drives with eyes fixed on the horizon. Her frown gives way to a broad smile when she realizes I'm watching her. I, in turn, smile. I hope that, behind our grown-up getup, behind our very different lives, the Delorme sisters are still there.

4:20 P.M.

A reception committee awaits us at Mima's house. Our dear Uncle Jean-Yves, aka the parking meter, is seated at the table with his wife Geneviève.

They watch us walk in, our arms loaded, without saying a word.

In the family, manners are no joke, and good manners dictate that it's the younger person that must greet the older one. It's the kind of training you swallow whole, and apply conscientiously throughout your life without ever questioning it.

"Hello uncle," I go, bending down to kiss him.

"Hi girls. Emma, it's been a long time."

My sister gives him a peck, while babbling:

"I couldn't come to the funeral, I wasn't expecting . . . I was afraid that . . . I'm so sorry . . . "

She blushes, her excuse makes no sense, no one expects such events. Unintentionally, Geneviève comes to her rescue:

"We received a message telling us the alarm had gone off. We had no idea you intended to come here."

"We felt like coming one last time," Emma explains. "Before the house is sold."

"You had the keys?" Jean-Yves queries.

"No, we came down the chimney," I reply. "Our reindeers watched over the sleigh outside the door."

My sister lowers her head, tries not to laugh.

"You might have warned us," snaps the parking-ticket machine. "We feared it was a burglary."

"We thought we could come to Mima's whenever we liked," I snap back.

"It's not Mima's anymore."

This last statement from Jean-Yves is so stark, even he seems surprised. Although, with his circumflex eyebrows, he always looks surprised. Must go back to the day he discovered, in anatomy class, that other skulls contain brains, too. Must have come as a shock to him, poor fellow.

"You can stay, of course," Geneviève tempers. "But make sure you don't damage the house, the buyer could deduct repair costs. A firm is coming next week to empty the property, so nothing must move between now and then."

I turn to my sister:

"D'you think we should cancel, for tomorrow?"

The bait might be blatant, but our uncle still dives on it:

"What are you planning?"

I shrug:

"Oh, nothing that bad, just a porn-movie shoot."

Emma bites her lip. Geneviève looks at me with commiseration:

"We're not your enemies, girls. We've always been there for you, we've done everything to help you."

I don't feel like laughing anymore. I refrain from flinging their so-called support back in their faces. It wouldn't take long, it can be summed up in a word: inexistent. We're not their nieces, we're the thorn in their side, a reflection of their guilt. The image we throw back at them is disgusting, so it's more bearable to tell themselves a different story. When all's said and done, it's a pretty banal form of human behavior, twisting the truth so it fits better into the scenery, deluding oneself with lies until one actually believes them.

"How long do you intend to stay?" Jean-Yves asks.

"A week," Emma informs him.

The parking meter and his wife look questioningly at each other, then, with the demeanor of those who want you to know they're generous without you realizing they want it to be known, they deign to let us spend this final week at our grandmother's house.

D addy and Mommy argued. We were eating at the Roulliers', Daddy's friends, and suddenly Mommy stood up and said "we're off" when there was still a chocolate charlotte to come for dessert. Daddy spoke quietly to her, Agathe cried, I sulked, but it was no good, we left. In the Renault 5, no one talked, except the radio. Daddy said a bad word when they announced that the humorist Pierre Desproges had died, I didn't dare ask a thing, must have been a friend of his.

We had to go straight to bed when we got home. Not even allowed to brush our teeth, first time ever! Our parents shut themselves in the kitchen, but we could hear them shouting from our room. Agathe got scared, she hates it when anyone shouts. I was mainly scared that they'd get divorced. It happened to Margaux's parents, and now she only sees her father during vacations, and she's gained half a brother (can't remember what it's called now.) I'd rather keep my father and just one sister, thanks.

We heard a door slam, Agathe started to cry, so she got into my bed. I read her The Famous Five so she wouldn't hear the shouting anymore and would think about something else, but in any case, it finally stopped and Agathe fell asleep. She kept moving about, I'm sure she's got ants in her pants, as Daddy says. At one stage, I got woken by something in my mouth; it was her foot.

When I got up, the shutters were still closed. I opened Daddy and Mummy's door, they were both there.

I'd forgotten how cold the water of the Atlantic is. The local pool isn't warm, but it has the decency not to freeze my toes off. I'd swim there every Tuesday morning, after dropping the kids off at the day-care center. It was the only day of the week they went, an arrangement reached after intense negotiations between my maternal guilt and my need for Me Time. One hour. That's the break I granted myself, shower and blow-dry included.

"Come on in, the water's lovely!"

Agathe makes as if to splash me, but something in my expression dissuades her. The waves are strong, they break close to the shore and crash up to the sand, gathering the beaming swimmers up in their foam. The spray tickles my nose. This is how I liked the sea to be. Raging, impetuous, unpredictable. Not offering itself to everyone but having to be earned. Mima taught us to understand the sea from an early age. At the start of every summer, she'd take us to the surfing club for lessons about the ocean. We became familiar with the tides, the wave formations, the currents, the troughs, the shore breaks. When very little, I'd been traumatized by the sight of a body brought out of the water by rescuers. A crowd had gathered around them as they tried cardiac massage. A helicopter finally arrived to take the person away. My father had told me not to look, but my curiosity got the better of me, and that faceless, colorless body haunted my nights for a long time. In my nightmares, the ocean would swallow me up before spitting my lifeless body back out onto the sand. The surfing classes taught me how to tackle the sea, and later, to love it. On January 1, I'd hang the calendar my mother bought from the mailman up on the wall of my room, in our two-bedroom apartment in Angoulême, and cross out each day between me and the summer vacation. Then, at last, those blissful days would return. Mima, my sister, being carefree, and the ocean.

"You're nearly there!" Agathe encourages me.

I advance warily in the freezing water, a centimeter at a time. My sister is already immersed, having dived straight in once she'd splashed her nape with water. She's so busy encouraging me, she doesn't notice the wave swelling up behind her.

"Come on, Emma! Come on, Emma!" she's chanting when the water smacks the back of her head and sends her flying in a roller of foam. I'm laughing so much that I don't have time to dive, so the wave drags me in turn, and I end up swirled in all directions, before landing on the shore in the most dignified of ways—both legs up in the air and one breast trying to escape. I look around for Agathe and spot her, just a bit further, trying to stand up with all the grace of an oyster.

"We're clearly not fifteen anymore!" she cries, laughing away. "My swimsuit tried to give me a colonoscopy."

"Mine collected sand in the 'hygienic gusset.' Never got what that thing was for, must remember to cut it off."

"Shall we go back in?"

Agathe doesn't wait for my reply, she charges back into the sea, leaping over any wavelets on the way. That first round finished me off, all I want is to lie on a towel and wait until my sister is ready to go home. But I just sit there, my backside in ten centimeters of water, watching her diving, jumping, floating like a log between waves. Dark clouds are gathering in the distance, buffeted by a new wind. They say that in the Basque Country, you can experience all four seasons in one day. Within minutes, it'll rain. Agathe gesticulates wildly at me. She was right, the water is lovely, I just needed to get used to it. I wait until a big wave comes and dies at my feet, and then run towards my sister before the next wave is born.

Bastien he take blue felt pen from me. I hit his face.

6:25 P.M.

She wants to go. I managed to drag it out for ten minutes, but when I tried for more, she looked daggers at me. I got back to my towel quicker than if I'd just brushed against a fin.

"We could go and have an aperitif at the covered market?"

Didn't see that coming. I imagined us set for an evening of TV and herbal tea, but now it's her suggesting we go out.

"Good idea!"

"Give me five minutes to dry off and then we'll hit the road?"

"No way, I'd rather we went dripping and half-naked."

I shake my head. She laughs. I'd lost the rhythm of our banter. It's a music I'm rediscovering. I flop down beside her, under the parasol. She takes out a towel and carefully dries herself.

"You don't like the sun anymore?" I ask.

"It's bad for the skin."

"Is that why you went off to live in the North Pole?"

"Strasbourg's not exactly the North Pole."

"You couldn't have gone any further from here."

"That was the idea."

Silence.

She lays her head on the ground and closes her eyes. Her thighs are marbled with fine veins. She's lost weight. She seems almost frail, yet she was always the stronger of us two.

"Shall we go?"

She stands up and slips her dress on over her retro swimsuit, which covers her shoulders and backside.

I do the same, covering up an urge to cry, too.

I didn't imagine our reunion being like this. I was naive enough to think that, if she wanted us to spend this week together, it was to get closer. What's the point of being side by side if you keep your distance?

We return to my scooter without a word. Here we are, back to the old sulking days, when we'd "quit talking." She was the best at that game, I'd just boil over. I'd shout, sob, hit, destroy. She always could hide her inner turmoil better than me.

"Drive slowly, please," she says, pulling on her helmet.

"You already told me that on the way here."

She'd wanted to come by car. I managed to dissuade her—finding a parking space would have taken hours. Once she'd accepted that we were going on my scooter, I was put through a rapid highway-code test. I rode as slowly as gravity allowed without us falling over, but despite that, she spent the journey clamped to my waist like a plunger to a sink. The return journey is less arduous—she opts to grip the handles—apart from her almost flying off at every hump.

"First dibs!" she shouts, as we arrive back at Mima's.

I haven't even taken my helmet off and she's already in the bathroom. I smoke a cig in the garden while waiting for her to shower. The terracotta ashtray is there, placed at the foot of the linden tree. It's empty, and noticing that is enough to make my eyes smart. I can still hear Mima bawling me out because it was overflowing with butts. As usual, she'd end up cleaning it out, and then putting it back exactly where I'd find it. Her problem wasn't that the ashtray overflowed, it was that I smoked. "You spent three weeks in an incubator so your lungs could develop," she'd often repeat to me, "and now you burn them with those filthy things. If we'd known, we'd have unplugged the machine, you'd have cost us less." I was used to this, and yet I'd chortle every time. She'd do anything to make us laugh.

The smoked cig is burning my fingers. I light another, in Mima's honor. I've spent my life thinking I'd never survive her death. For as long as I've loved her, I've feared losing her. When I was little, every time the phone rang late at night, every time she didn't answer immediately, every time my mother frowned upon hearing some news, I was certain she had died. I didn't think it, I *knew* it. I wept over her lifeless body, attended her funeral, felt her absence intensely, and then I'd find out that she was well, that it was something else, and I'd suffocate with joy, thank heaven, fate, the phone, my mother, all that I could thank, and life would suddenly become delightful, wonderful, amazing. A shrink once told me that hypochondriacs take news of a serious illness the best. They practice so much for it that, when it happens, they're ready. But it doesn't work for me. I may have rehearsed for it all my life, but I'm not ready for Mima's absence. I can't see how the world can keep turning without its axis. Can't see how I could ever recover from losing the only person who has never let me down.

Emma comes out of the house and joins me. Water is dripping from her short hair onto her dress.

"It's all yours," she goes.

I stub out my cigarette but stay sitting on the grass. She observes me, then sits down beside me. We stay silent for a moment, facing the house that harbors quite a few of our memories. Emma lays her head on my shoulder and murmurs:

"Did you see? The poppies are out."

We arrived at Mima and Papi's after a long drive. Agathe peed in the car, she didn't want to go to the bathroom before setting off. She was crying because she was soaking wet, but had to wait until we could stop at some services. She was hurting my ears, but then Daddy thought of putting on the Chantal Goya cassette, and that calmed her down.

I saw the poppies as soon as we entered Mima's garden. We'd planted the seeds with her during the Easter vacation. We were allowed to pick them so me and my sister did two bunches, one for Mima and one for Mommy, even though she's not here.

It's the first time she hasn't come to Anglet with us, she told us just before we left that she had some important work to finish. She gave us some shell-shaped sweets for the journey, but Daddy didn't want us eating them in the car and making a mess everywhere. Agathe didn't want to leave her, and neither did I, but Mommy promised to join us there soon and gave us a big hug. She smelt of patchouli.

We ate under the linden tree, a rice salad with cherry tomatoes from the garden. Agathe ate loads of them, and even stole one off my plate, so for that I took some cheese off hers.

I wanted to go to the beach, but we had to wait until we'd digested our food. It's always like that, I don't really get what difference it makes, but Mommy once said that when you're a child, you don't need to understand, just to obey.

The water was lovely, but the waves were too big, so I played at the edge with Agathe and Mima, while Daddy and Papi swam. We built a splendid castle, and I dug a moat right around it, and

Mima collected some shells to decorate it, but we couldn't show it
to Daddy because Agathe jumped on it and destroyed everything.
I threw sand at her face and she threw the rake at my head. Mima
asked us to kiss and make up, and after we played at running faster
than the little waves at the edge, which was funny, especially when
Agathe fell over.

Mima wouldn't stop kissing us and telling us she loved us. Now
I think about it, I believe it was because she knew what was going
to happen that evening.

When we got back to the house, I ran to the bathroom shouting
"First dibs!" and Agathe cried, so tomorrow I'll let her shower first.
When I came out, Uncle Jean-Yves, Auntie Geneviève, and our
cousins were there. I was pleased, but not for long because Daddy
took Agathe and me into his bedroom from when he was little and
said he had to talk to us about something important. We were even
allowed to eat the shell sweets, but I didn't finish them because he
spoilt everything. It was a lovely day, and now it's the day Daddy
and Mommy got divorced.

D addy comes to the house to collect us, but Mommy doesn't want him to. They shout loud, I put my fingers in my ears so I can't hear.

Mommy says he's nasty. I think Daddy's nice.

I get into Emma's bed. She pushes me away, but then she says okay and I fall asleep with her and Firefly.

7:43 P.M.

I hadn't been to the place for what seemed a lifetime. Biarritz's covered market hasn't changed, the terraces of the bars and restaurants overflow with families, couples, colleagues, and friends, all mingling into a festive hubbub. We opt for a standing table, Agathe asks what I'd like to drink, and goes to order it at the bar. On her way, she greets two people, and the waitress hugs her. This place is her territory.

"It's crazy. I feel like I'm still twenty, when I'm approaching my forties."

"You're telling me, I'm already floundering in mine."

The waitress puts down two glasses of wine and some tapas.

"To the Delorme sisters," goes Agathe, raising her glass.

"To us."

Silence sets in. My sister wolfs down the sheep's cheese brochettes, I tackle the duck fillet on bread. I don't know whether we have nothing to say to each other, or too much and don't know where to start. There's a five-year hole in our story.

"D'you have a photo of Alice?" she asks me.

I take out my phone and pull up a picture of my daughter on the screen. Agathe takes the phone and scrolls through the photos:

"She's wonderful. I wonder who she gets that from."

"No doubt from her aunt. I warn you, there are hundreds of photos."

"Have you gone soft?"

"Totally. I have to stop myself from gobbling her up. She has quite a temper, often reminds me of you."

She smiles.

"And Sacha? He must have grown so much!"

I open the file containing photos of my son, and hand the phone back to her:

"He's just celebrated his tenth birthday. His shoe size is the same as mine, and he's up to my chin."

"It goes by so fast . . . Do they get on well?"

"Really well. I was apprehensive, what with seven years between them, but the big brother is very protective, and the little sister adores her brother. They do sometimes fall out, sure, but they have a really lovely relationship. I hope it'll last . . . "

Agathe downs several gulps of wine, then lights a cigarette:

"Not much is stronger than the relationship between brother and sister. Try as you might, you can't just get rid of a shared childhood like that, it clings to you."

I don't get time to react; a tall, dark guy invites himself to our table and drapes his arm heavily around my sister's shoulders:

"I've been watching you since earlier, and I absolutely must ask you a question."

"You must also take your hands off my shoulders, pronto," Agathe warns.

"Were you in the war?" the guy asks, very seriously.

"The war? No, why?" she asks, surprised.

"Because you're a bombshell."

I stop myself from laughing. The punchline is cringeworthy.

Agathe frees herself from his grip and retorts, quick as a flash:

"Clear off if you don't want a ringside seat at the explosion. Tick tock, tick tock."

The oaf is amused, impervious to his target's annoyance.

"Come on, stay cool!" he urges. "You're too stunning to be snooty. What's your name?"

"Monique."

"Pleased to meet you, Monique. What d'you do for a living?"

"I'm a fakir, always have a bed of nails with me, got an ass like Gruyère."

I spit my wine back out. As for the guy, he's not laughing at all now. I put my hand on his shoulder so he notices my presence:

"Monsieur, could you leave us in peace, please?"

"Well hello there!" he replies. "You look less dumb than your friend!"

Agathe says nothing more, she knows how much I hate scenes. I can see her closing up, I fear her losing it. No one's noticed us, I'd like that to continue, and yet I can feel myself boiling over:

"Monsieur, my sister has made it clear to you that she doesn't want to talk to you. So would you, your sweaty armpits, and your farm-raised mussel charisma kindly go and look elsewhere."

Agathe's jaw drops. The guy shakes his head and makes to leave, with a nasty laugh:

"I was just doing you a favor," he says, disdainfully. "You can't get chatted up very often."

He turns on his heel and disappears into the crowd. At that moment, the waitress puts two fresh glasses of wine on the table. Agathe raises hers:

"To the Delorme sisters, and to farm-raised mussels!"

Daddy's got a new sweetheart. Mommy doesn't want me calling her Mommy, but anyhow, she's called Martine. She bought me a Fairy Barbie with the dress that shines in the dark, she's nice.

Her son is called David, he's a big boy.

Daddy built a shelf, with his machine that hurts my ears, and he put my favorite books on it, the ones about a lamb and a leopard. He reads the words and I look at the pictures. I have a bedroom all to myself, and Emma's even got a bathroom.

Daddy picked a video in the store. It's the story of a rabbit called Roger and a lady with orange hair called Jessica, but then a nasty man puts a nice shoe in some stuff and it disappears. I cry, so Daddy turns off the TV, says sorry, that I'm too little, and then we play jackstraws.

At night I'm too scared on my own, so I get into Emma's bed. She doesn't say anything now, I get into her bed every night at Daddy's, she budges up a bit, and then I can fall asleep.

Later, Daddy gives us a surprise, we go to the place with lots of dogs in cages. Daddy has hidden a leash in his pocket and the man gives us a dog that was waiting for us. He's called Snoopy, he's brown, and I'm happy. He's funny, Emma says "sit" and he sits, his tail is always wagging, and he comes everywhere with us, even when I go to pee. Daddy doesn't want him up on the sofa, so me and Emma sit on the carpet, and Daddy comes down beside us.

I'm sad when Daddy takes us back. He just keeps talking, but his eyes are all wet. I say bye-bye to him with my hand and he *drives off, and Mommy opens the door and she says she missed us, and she kisses us, and she asks if Martine was there, and she puts Fairy Barbie into the trash can.*

10:13 P.M.

Emma didn't want to admire the sunset. I'd forgotten that it's not her thing. As for me, it's one of my favorite spectacles, along with Brad Pitt's face. I've watched *Legends of the Fall* so many times, my name should appear on the credits. Particularly the moment when Brad, having been away for years, reappears, galloping, in the majestic Montana setting, escorted by wild horses. I'd have gladly auditioned to play his nag.

"I'm off to bed," Emma announces, opening Mima's gate.

"Already?"

"The drive here did me in, and I still have the bed to make. Can I take Dad's room?"

"If you like. I'll sleep in uncle's."

She goes up the first few steps, then stops:

"Good night, little sister."

"Good night, big sister."

For a moment, I get the impression Emma wants to say something more to me, but she carries on up the stairs.

I go to the back of the house, root out the cushions in the storeroom, and lie on the swing seat. The sky is studded with stars—stare at it without blinking and you can make out the Milky Way.

Little sister. That's what I am. I was born a little sister, and I'll die a little sister. I'm firmly convinced that one's position among siblings affects, even determines, the adult one becomes. I'd doubtless be different if I'd been the elder sister. The first child traces the path, fills all the space, sucks up all the attention.

The parents focus on that child's very existence, the anxieties surrounding that child, the impact of all those first times. For many, the family is born with the first child. Those that follow enlarge it, the first starts it. So the firstborn assumes an importance and a responsibility that the siblings who follow can't know. They arrive in an occupied space. The attention is divided, the anxieties are eased, the first times already experienced. They have a model as they develop, whether they emulate it or oppose it. Their character defines itself in reaction to, in comparison with: they make more noise or less waves, are more this or less that. I don't know which position is the more enviable. Each has its advantages and drawbacks. I only know that I'm the second one, the last one, the little one, the one who came after, and that I've felt it deeply, viscerally, all my life.

I light a cig and turn on my phone. Mathieu hasn't replied to my message. He's seen it, or so the little blue symbol at the bottom of the screen tells me. In my mind, I compose the next one I'll write to him before forcing myself not to send it. My pride went missing at the same time as him. I'm aware that I'm doing myself no favors by bombarding him with pleading messages, but I can't help it. I'm fiddling frantically with the beads of my bracelet when Emma's head appears at the upstairs window.

"Agathe, come and see!"

"Coming."

I stub my cigarette out on the ground—I can almost hear Mima cursing—and join my sister in her room. She's facing her phone. On the screen, a little girl and a curly-haired boy.

"Children, say hello to your aunt."

"Hello, auntie!"

Sacha can't have any memory of me, he was five the last time he saw me. Alice only knows me through the words of others. It's facing them, so grown, that I become aware of the time that's passed. That is, an absence of five years. A pregnancy, those first steps, all of elementary school, grazed knees, drawings on the

wall, wobbly teeth, bedtime stories, shoes on the wrong feet, fun-
fairs, lisped words. One sure gets through some memories over
five years.

I exchange a few words with them, they're very natural, I'm
awkward, I laugh a bit too loudly, don't want them imagining that
I'm moved.

Alex decides to join in, on the screen:

"Hi Agathe! Good to see you."

"Same!"

He, too, has gotten through quite a few things over these five
years, including nearly all of his hair.

"When are you coming to see us?" he asks.

"Oh yes!" Sacha exclaims. "Come and see us at home!"

"Is she coming later?" Alice asks.

I laugh once again:

"No, sweetie, but I'll come another day. Promise!"

The phone shakes slightly. I take it from my sister's hand and
prop it up against a pile of clothes on the shelf. I ask the children
questions, my brother-in-law his news, I see Emma in her role of
mother, of wife, when I mainly know her in that of sister. Then
Alex announces that it's already late, that the little ones must go
to bed, and the screen goes dark, and my sister whispers that
she'd like to go to bed, too, and kisses me, and the door closes. I
return to the swing seat, the cigarette, and the bracelet of beads,
thinking how, despite the screen between us, despite the distance
between us, that thing I was just part of, for a few moments, was
very like a family.

Dear Journal de Mickey,

I saw that readers can write to you to ask you questions, and I've got one. Since I watched The Big Blue, I dream of working with dolphins. I'd like to know what I should study. I hope I'll get an answer (I wrote to Star Club magazine, they didn't reply.)

Emma

PS: I'm not mad on Donald Duck, he's always annoyed.

7:10 A.M.

I can't sleep. Keeps happening, lately. Dark thoughts drag me from sleep and, to escape them, I have to get up.

This used to be Agathe's thing. Anxiety, her territory. Mine was being practical. Emma can sort out tricky situations. Emma will straighten things out. Emma is so mature. I wore the outfit that I'd been dressed in without asking myself whether it fitted me. At forty-two, I'm discovering how cramped I feel in it.

I can hear Agathe snoring, through the partition wall. She got to bed late. I heard the front-door handle at two in the morning. I get dressed and go downstairs, avoiding the creaky step. The sun, only just awake, sneaks through the slits of the shutters. I open them, the morning freshness fills the sitting room, and I flop onto the armchair.

This was Mima's place. For sixty-two years, she sat here every morning. She read hundreds of books here, knitted numerous cable sweaters, wrote poems, graded her pupils' work, peeled potatoes, rocked her sons, mourned one of them, did my hair. On the pedestal table beside the armrest, I recognize the notebook she'd write all her recipes in. She'd gotten most of them from her mother, who'd gotten them from her own mother, and the notebook was meant for us. She was of a time when women did the cooking; it would never have occurred to her to pass the recipes on to our male cousins. I turn the pages, some stained from frying or icing, and each recipe summons a memory. Spaghetti with meatballs, couscous, polpettone, oreillettes, tiramisu, mias, ricotta ravioli, farfalle with zucchini, lasagne, campanare, kiwi ice cream, orange cake . . . I can see her once more, apron tied around waist, in her little kitchen with no countertop. I must have been sixteen when she decided she had to teach me how to make gnocchi. I was keener to go to the beach with the girl from next door, but I sensed that this passing-on was important to her. Magnanimously, I agreed to give Mima some time, telling my friend I'd join her soon, convinced that in an hour, at most, I'd be done. Four hours later, the dish was ready, Mima was delighted, my sister was starving, and I was ready to slit my wrists with onion peel. My grandmother stuck a fork into some gnocchi and popped it into my mouth before I had time to react. I chewed, gazing heavenwards, then declared that, truly, it was just as good as the vacuum-packed gnocchi from the supermarket.

The final page of the notebook is covered in shaky handwriting, in contrast to that, steady and clear, of the first recipes. Seeing this breaks my heart. In my little girl's mind, my grandmother had always been an old person. I became aware quite recently that when I was born, she wasn't even fifty. No doubt my children see me as I saw her. I wasn't there as she grew old. I missed her last years. We'd call each other regularly, I'd send her photos, but I didn't visit. I thought I had time, never imagined she might actually disappear one day. She was the only person never to let us down. She was the dependable figure, the unchanging point of reference. When I ran away, I turned my grandmother into collateral damage.

I need to get out for some air.

I grab my bag, my car keys, and leave the house.

7:42 A.M.

I don't know how I ended up here. I drove aimlessly, carried along by memories of bygone summers. The ocean is at my feet, the water lapping at my toes. It's calm today. The sun warms my back, I lift my dress and walk a few steps. The beach is almost deserted. An old man ambles towards the water, followed by a flock of seagulls. He's in swim shorts and has shoulder-length white hair. I recognize him, he's been part of the Basque landscape for a long time. Every morning, come rain, or wind, or snow, he arrives to feed the birds. He plunges his hand into his bag, and the ballet commences: he throws the food into the water, the gulls dive on it, one of them, being swifter, snatches it and flies off with its meal, while the others wheel around the man. The story goes that he only likes animals, that he hurls insults at anyone who dares speak to him. I avoid doing so and watch the spectacle in silence.

I'm up to my thighs in water. A bigger wave is forming in the distance. I turn around to beat a retreat, try to run, but the current holds me back, my strides more like running on the spot, I don't give up, I use my arms, too, I propel myself, I strain forward, and go under headfirst.

The old man has turned in my direction and is staring at me. Smiling, I give him a wave.

"Fuck off!" he shouts back at me, charmingly.

Not a wave on the horizon anymore. I let my body float on the surface and stretch out my arms. My ears are underwater, all I can hear now is the muffled silence. The sun warms my face. The swell of the sea rocks me and instantly soothes me. I breathe in slowly, I breathe out slowly, several times, then I get out of the water before a fresh lot of waves start up.

I stay there for about ten minutes, watching a lady walk her dog and a young man prepare to surf. My hair dries fast, one of the things I appreciate about wearing it short. I gather up my bag and shoes and make my way back to the parking lot. My sodden dress weighs a ton and clings to my legs. The man is still on the sand, even though the gulls, having got what they wanted, have deserted him.

"Have a nice day, monsieur!"

He looks at me as if I'd seriously offended him, and replies in the same tone:

"Screw you, bag of shit!"

I'm top of my class. I was already top last month, but I couldn't believe it because Céline's better at capital letters than me. The teacher makes me pick a picture out of the box. I've already got all of them, they're the ones you get in boxes of cocoa, but I don't say anything—I'll give it to Céline.

Daddy and Mommy will be pleased, and Emma will give me her slot-in record player, she promised she would. She won't need it anymore seeing as she's getting a radio cassette player and recorder. She said she'd also give me the Roch Voisine record—I know the words by heart. Mommy loves it, too, but she prefers Patrick Bruel.

The principal comes into the classroom and calls out my name. Everyone looks at me, I don't understand, I hope it's to give me another reward. I follow her, I'm a bit scared, and I see Mommy in the schoolyard. She's wearing her green coat and her eyes are red, she cries when she sees me. Maybe it's because she's pleased. She tries to speak but can't, so it's the principal who tells me that Daddy's had an accident.

Mommy wasn't sure if we should go to the funeral, but Mima said it was important.

There aren't many people there. The only funeral I've seen is the comedian Coluche's on the TV, and there were loads more people. And yet my father was kind, too.

Mima won't stop stroking our hair. Papi is holding her arm, she almost fell over as she entered the church. The priest got Daddy's name wrong: he called him Alain, when his name is Michel. It made my cousin Laurent laugh, and he couldn't stop so Auntie Geneviève took him outside.

It goes on for ages, it's cold, you have to stand up, sit down, stand up, sit down, and the priest only talks about Jesus when it's Daddy who's died.

Mommy cries a lot, maybe she still loved him, in fact.

Martine is at the back of the church with David. I didn't dare say hello to her, Mommy's unhappy enough as it is.

There's one minute to think about Daddy, and all that comes to me is last Sunday. We were watching Baywatch, and at one stage Mitch Buchannon said he'd found some bullet holes in a boat. Daddy started laughing, I didn't understand why, so he explained that it also meant assholes, and we laughed together. Agathe wanted to be told, too, but Daddy didn't want to because she's too young. He asked me not to tell Mommy about it, I promised, but I told her all the same, and she said it wasn't very smart of him.

We come out of the church and some men arrive to collect the coffin. We walk to the cemetery, it's just nearby. The sky is orange, *the sun is setting, and for the first time I find it sad. My right hand is frozen. In my left one, since Daddy died, I've been holding the hand of my little sister.*

9:00 A.M.
I sleep too much. Keeps happening, lately. Sleep drags me away from dark thoughts; to escape them, I have to go back to sleep. It's the only place I get any relief from the anxiety and gloom.

My phone alarm gives me a start. I half-open one eye to press the right key, the one that lets me snooze again for nine minutes.

9:09 A.M.
I must get up.
I'm so cozy in bed.
Go on, just a bit longer.

9:18 A.M.
Nine minutes is no big deal.

9:27 A.M.
One last time.
Promise.

9:36 A.M.
One very last time.
Very last time, very, very last time, very, very last time.
Shit, it's stuck in my head.

9:45 A.M.
A bit of willpower, Agathe.
A.

Bit.

Of.

9:54 A.M.

Emma bursts into my room and opens the shutters.

"Time to get up in here! It's almost 10 o'clock and we've got a packed schedule!"

I pull the sheet over my face, groaning.

"What schedule?"

"We're going to the Rhune."

I suddenly sit up:

"By train?"

"Absolutely not. We've talked long enough about doing it on foot, now's the time."

I lie back down.

"Good night, Emma."

She leaves the room, laughing:

"Come on, get ready, and wear suitable shoes. I'm waiting for you downstairs!"

The Rhune is a Pyrenean mountain you can see from Anglet. Mima took us up several times aboard the legendary 1920s rack-railway train. From the summit, the view over the Basque Country and the coast is extraordinary, but being about as sporty as a slug, my reaching it on a stretcher can't be ruled out.

11:52 A.M.

I don't know where she gets this power from. She always manages to win me over. It was decided, it was out of the question that I go up the Rhune on foot. And here I am, in my most comfortable sneakers, flask in hand, tackling the hiking path.

"You okay?" she asks me.

"Marvelous. Best day of my life."

"Don't worry, we'll go at your pace."

"That would make getting there unlikely, my pace is in neutral."

She laughs. She's always been the most sporty. She started gymnastics in first grade and did one meet after another until high school. As for me, I tried judo, dance, athletics, handball and swimming, and the findings of this exhaustive research are conclusive: sport doesn't want me.

11:58 A.M.
Still alive. STOP.

12:11 P.M.
It's quite enjoyable, in the end. We walk slowly, so we can admire the surroundings. We stopped a minute to stroke some Pottok ponies. It's me who had to get us walking again, or we'd still be there.

12:18 P.M.
Something weird is going on. My watch says we've been walking for twenty-six minutes, but my legs are screaming that we've been walking for twenty-six hours. One of the two is lying, I'm inclined to trust my body.

12:22 P.M.
My sister's watch says the same as mine. Either there's a solidarity between watches, or they're telling the truth.

12:30 P.M.
The more one wants time to pass quickly, the more it drags. It's contrary. I'm sure it's a Scorpio.

12:31 P.M.
We've just been overtaken by a group of retirees equipped with poles. They greeted us, I refrained from turning them into brochettes.

12:32 P.M.

Emma suggests I take a break. I deduce from that I look like I'm dying, but I haven't the strength to take offence. We sit on a rock away from the path.

"If you like, we'll take the train to go back down," she suggests, generously.

"It's that or the emergency services, your choice."

"I admit I wasn't expecting it to be this exhausting."

I lay my hand on her shoulder:

"It's true, it must be tough at your age."

She pretends to be offended:

"Watch out, you'll soon be joining me as a fortysomething!"

"Don't remind me. I'm counting on you to support me. I'll need someone to help me choose my diapers and gruel."

She bursts out laughing:

"Bitch!"

"See, you're already going gaga."

12:45 P.M.

The old girl's taking her revenge, she's quickened the pace.

1:00 P.M.

"Want another break?" Emma asks. "I made some sandwiches."

We settle down in the shade of a fir tree, and I must admit, the panorama is nicer than the view from my kitchen. The Basque Country rolls out all its variations of green, clouds bob here and there, and some not-that-wild cows graze just meters away from us. Most striking of all is the silence. Apart from the steps of hikers and the bells around the cows' necks, there's not a sound. It's when you can't hear the noise anymore that you notice that's it's always there. Even the din in my head is on hold.

Emma hands me a sandwich:

"Cured ham," she announces.

"I'm still a vegetarian."

"Just kidding! I made you one with Roquefort and walnuts."

I loathe Roquefort. I loathe all strong cheeses in general, but Roquefort even more than the rest. Just knowing it's the mold that gives it that taste can make me sick. She must have forgotten that. And yet, touched by her gesture, I bite into the sandwich (making sure to eat mainly bread) and pretend I'm loving it.

1:23 P.M.

I've tried to find the motivation to set off again, since finishing the only mouthful of sandwich I managed to swallow. Emma thought I didn't like it, I claimed that the chocolatine I ate just before leaving had cut my appetite. She closes her bag and slings it on her back:

"Know what Mima would say?"

"That you have crap ideas."

"Stop it, I'm sure you're forcing yourself to be negative when you're actually loving this climb."

"You've seen right through me," I reply, gloomily. "So, what would Mima say?"

"That one mustn't do anything strenuous while digesting."

I look at her, not daring to understand; she confirms it:

"And also, it's too hot for all this nonsense."

I almost throw my arms around her, but guilt holds me back.

"Emma, I'm finding it tough, but you know me: I always exaggerate. I don't want you depriving yourself for my sake."

She assures me it's fine, I assure her I'll keep going, she insists she can totally skip it, I insist I can totally manage it, and after an unlikely turnaround in the situation, where I'm almost begging her to scale this goddam mountain, it's she who wins yet again, and we head back down.

I'm seven today. I got an envelope from Mima, like every year. Inside there was a pearl, which I put away with the others, and a poem written on a postcard with horses on it.

Mommy said I'd reached the age of reason, but that didn't mean I was always right.

I was allowed to invite five friends to the house: Caroline, Olivia, Aziza, Marjorie, and Céline, but afterwards I uninvited Céline because she got a higher grade than me in dictation.

Marjorie gave me some Polly Pocket dolls—she's my new best friend.

We haven't got a garden anymore. Apparently, Mommy couldn't pay for the house any longer, so now we live in an apartment on the third floor. Maybe that's why she didn't want to take Snoopy when Daddy died, and she let him go back to the shelter.

My friends wanted to go and play on the parking lot down below, but Mommy didn't want us to, she said we mustn't hang around outside because of the grown-ups who harm children.

She let us use the mini music system and lent us all her scarves and high-heel shoes; she even put lipstick on us. We dressed up and danced, and Emma played her favorite music ("Rhythm Is a Dancer" by Snap!) and showed us all the moves, and it was good fun.

Mommy had forgotten to buy the cake, I was sad, I cried, so she told me off and said that I wasn't being nice, that she was allowed to make mistakes, that I was never happy. It's not true, I'm even very happy sometimes. After, she came and gave me a kiss, and made some pancakes. I'd never eaten such delicious ones and she said it was thanks to her secret ingredient (I don't know what it's called, but it's what she always drinks from her bottle).

It really was a great birthday, except that Daddy wasn't there.

I can hear Agathe crying. At first I thought it was the neighbor's cat, it's forever meowing at night, but I'm sure it's her. I don't know if I should go to her, I've got a Bio test tomorrow and I must get a good grade. Last time I got zero because I didn't manage to dissect the frog. Instead, I puked on Madame Rabot's shoes, which she wasn't thrilled about. Mommy said that if my report for the second term isn't good, I won't go to Mima and Papi's this summer, and that is just out of the question.

She is crying a lot, though.

I get up on tiptoes, Mommy's watching Ciel, mon mardi!, she mustn't hear me. I make my way thanks to the light from the streetlamps outside. For a while now, I haven't been closing the shutters.

Agathe is hugging her firefly and the head is lit up (the firefly's, not Agathe's).

"What's up?" I whisper to her.

"I can't sleep."

"That's no big deal! You mustn't get worked up about that."

I start to leave, but she tells me she's scared.

"Scared of what?"

"Of earthquakes."

I laugh a bit, but she cries even more. I sit on her bed and explain that there are no earthquakes in Angoulême.

"What about volcanoes?"

"No volcanoes, either, Gagathe."

She tells me that her teacher told them the story of the people in a village who all died under lava, because of a volcano that erupted over just one night.

"I don't want to die, Emma, I'm too little!"

"Don't move, I'll be back."

I tiptoe back to my room and return with my atlas. There's a page on volcanoes, I read it out loud, she's a bit reassured. I continue with the page on earthquakes, and by the end she's stopped crying altogether. I stay with her a bit longer, then go back to my bed, because tomorrow I've got the Bio test.

4:49 P.M.

"I'd really like to know where the cat's gone."

Emma, engrossed in reading the poems in Mima's notebook, just shrugs. She never knew Robert Redford, our grandmother adopted him three or four years ago.

She was on her way to the Quintaou market when she found him, lying on the pavement. He'd clearly been run over by someone who hadn't bothered to stop. He was in a bad way. She settled him in her basket and took him to the local vet, who told her the cat was neither microchipped nor tattooed, and in the absence of official owners, she'd have to pay for the consultation and treatment. Mima hesitated: her love for other people's pets was limited by her bank account, which was in a more pitiful state than the cat. But the look in the creature's eyes won her over. She never got to the market in the end. The cat had an X-ray and a blood test, which showed nothing serious, but part of his tail had to be removed, and his paw pads and head stitched up. Despite the vet letting her pay in three instalments, she had to dip into her teacher's pension. The cat convalesced at home with her, she put notices up at all the surrounding businesses, and, after a few days without hearing from anyone claiming ownership, she decided to call the cat Robert Redford: "He cost me a fortune, but being able to say I'm Robert Redford's mistress is a small consolation."

"When did he disappear?" Emma asks.

"When Mima went to hospital. I'd come to feed him every day and spend some time with him—he'd show up when he heard my scooter—and then one day he stopped coming."

"Did you look for him?"

"A bit, in the neighborhood, but then Mima died and that was all I could think about. I'd like to find him, I'd keep him at my place. I can't bear the thought of him being abandoned. She loved him a lot, looked after him like a kid."

"I can imagine, I saw he had a basket in every room and a giant cat tree!" goes my sister.

"That's not the worst of it."

I tell her about the lengths our grandmother went to so Robert Redford wouldn't go outside at night, her anxiety when she heard cats fighting, the grooming brush she'd massage him with every evening, and the nights when she'd refrain from going to the bathroom because monsieur was sleeping peacefully on her stomach.

"We have to find him!" she decides.

5:30 P.M.

We called all the shelters in the area, the pound, and the town hall. They all seemed surprised that we were looking for a cat that had been missing for more than three months, and none came up with one matching our description. He's easy to recognize: all black, except the lower legs, as if wearing socks.

Emma suggests we ask Madame Garcia, the neighbor. I can't stand her, I'd rather have a semi-trailer in place of my ass than speak to her, but my sister insists: she doesn't dare go there alone. I understand her—I'm the sort who gets lost rather than ask the way, who practices what I need to say before making a call, who doesn't enter a boutique if I'm the only customer. A shrink informed me that this is social anxiety disorder. Which didn't surprise me that much. Even when I was little, I'd sometimes wet myself while reciting a poem from the blackboard. No one suspects this about me, I put them off the scent, most people think I'm always totally at ease. In reality, behind my armor, I just want to disappear as soon as the focus is on me. Emma's the same. In quite a few respects, we're totally unalike. She thinks ahead and is organized, whereas I'm laid-back and chaotic, but a few character traits leave no doubt as to our shared childhood and blood.

Madame Garcia doesn't immediately recognize us.

"I don't need anything, thank you!" she goes, before closing the door.

We persevere and, upon hearing our name, she comes to open the gate to us. Madame Garcia has been Mima's neighbor forever, if forever means as far back as I can remember. She's younger than Mima, closer to our mother's age.

"Well fancy that! I wouldn't have recognized you! Well, the little one, I do see her from time to time, from a distance."

The little one, that's me. I muster a smile that's as convincing as my hatred for her allows. I find it regrettable that there's not a facial expression or gesture to indicate to someone that one doesn't like them. Apart from a headbutt, I mean.

Madame Garcia hasn't seen Robert Redford.

"And I'm delighted about that," she feels obliged to add. "That cat used to scratch about in my flowerbeds, it destroyed everything. Anyhow, do come in, have a cool drink!"

"That's kind, but we have to get going," Emma replies.

Furthermore, we don't want to. But I refrain from thinking that too loud, just in case it can be heard.

"Go on, just for five minutes!" the leech insists. "Joachim is here, he'll be pleased to see you."

One more reason to cut and run. Joachim is the last person I feel like seeing, but Emma has never been good at resisting polite insistence, and we end up following the neighbor through her lush garden. In the sitting room, Monsieur Garcia has dozed off in front of the TV.

"Jojo!" Madame Garcia calls out to her son, with no consideration for her husband, who wakes with a start. "The little neighbors are here!"

Emma sits down, I prefer to remain standing. Joachim turns up and greets us as if he really were pleased to see us. I'm surprised to see him with gray hair and lines around his eyes. In the end, where we most notice ourselves ageing is on other people's bodies.

"What are you up to, girls?" Joachim asks.

"I'm an elementary school teacher," Emma replies. "Grades 4 and 5."

He turns to me:

"And you?"

"I'm a fakir, always have a bed of nails with me, got an—"

"She's a support worker," Emma interrupts me, embarrassed.

"That doesn't surprise me, of you," the neighbor comments. "I bet you look after children."

"Wrong," I reply. "I didn't want to have time to become attached, so I chose old people."

"Do you still draw?"

"No. And you, what do you do?"

I care as much about his answer as about my first fungal infection; the guy deserves every insult there is from me, but that wouldn't be the best way to prove to Emma that I've changed. So, showing a César-worthy interest, I listen to Joachim talking about his life as a statistician.

T homas Martel French kissed me. It was gross. I'd even rather eat snails. I knew it was going to happen, he's wanted to go out with me since last year, but I didn't want to while I had braces. The orthodontist removed them a few days ago. She wanted me to keep wearing them a bit longer, but I'm done, it's been three years, she puts it off at every appointment, and I'm sick of laughing with my mouth closed. The worst is at night, I have to wear a kind of brace with headgear—if I ran into Freddy Krueger, it's him who'd be scared.

Thomas told me to meet him at the fun fair. Margaux and Karima came with me, we walked there, cutting through the tennis courts. I put on some perfume (Démon by Eau Jeune.) I was asking myself loads of questions: what direction to turn my tongue, should I close my eyes, do I put my arms around his neck or his waist, and what if I dribble, like when I'm asleep at night? The girls were reassuring me, but when we got there, I almost turned back.

He was waiting for me behind the truck for the bumper cars. We just said hello and, boom, we were French kissing. I didn't even have time to think about all my questions, and afterwards, Margaux told me I'd kept my eyes open and arms stuck to my sides. All I remember is that I stopped breathing.

Thomas held my hand all afternoon, I don't know which of us was sweating, but it felt clammy.

Mom told me to get home at six o'clock, it's twenty past when I arrive at our building. It's Karima's fault, we had to find some chewing gum so her parents wouldn't smell that she'd been smoking. I wind my watch back twenty minutes and walk up the three floors.

"You're late," Mom says.

I show her my Casio:

"No, look, I'm exactly on time."

I don't see it coming. Her hand slams against my cheek, my ear starts ringing.

"Do you take me for a damn fool, Emma?"

"No, Mom, I promise you."

"Do you want another slap?"

"No."

"Well, don't lie to me. Apologize and go to your room."

"Sorry."

"Sorry who?"

"Sorry Mom."

"Go."

I run to my room and throw myself onto my bed. I'm crying so much I don't hear Agathe come in. She sits down beside me and strokes my head:

"Need to put a cool washcloth on it. Made me feel much better, the last time."

Mommy's coming to collect us this evening. The summer vacation is over. We spent the two months at Mima and Papi's. Mima said that's how it'll always be. Mommy agrees. I say nothing because I don't want to upset Mommy, but I don't really feel like going home. I'd like summer to last all year. I couldn't even finish the Italian ice cream, my throat's that tight.

For our last day, we all go to the beach together. There's Mima, Papi, Uncle Jean-Yves, Auntie Geneviève, and our cousins. Jérôme's my favorite. He's a year older than me, while Laurent is the same age as Emma. The waves are big, and although I remember all we learned at the surfing classes, I prefer to stay at the edge. Jérôme stays with me, we build a sandcastle, we play with the rackets, I keep hitting the ball too long or too wide, we have a good laugh.

Emma's swimming in a T-shirt, everyone's asking her why, but I know why, it's because her boobs are growing and she's ashamed. She told me at the beginning of summer. I'd really like to have big boobs, and sometimes, in my room, I even put on one of Mommy's bras stuffed with socks.

The lifeguards blow their whistles and wave their arms, and two of them run into the water. The sun's in my eyes, I can't see that clearly, but someone has swum out too far and can't get back. Jérôme tells me it's Emma. I look everywhere for her, but can't see her, I think he's right, it really is her, I don't feel too good, I can barely breathe, my head starts spinning, my heart makes a noise in my ears, I'm scared, she's my sister, I love her too much, I don't want her to drown, Mima hugs me and tries to calm me down, but I

can't, I'm shaking all over, everything goes dark, I feel like puking,
I'm hot, I can't hear a thing anymore.

When I come to, I'm under the parasol, and Emma's holding
my hand. She's alive, I throw myself into her arms. "I love you,
Emma, I love you!" She tells me it wasn't her in the water, she was
at the edge, not far from us, watching the scene. Mima explains to
me that I had a panic attack. I'm not really sure what that is, but I
didn't like it.

On the way back, Uncle Jean-Yves lends me twenty centimes to
buy myself some mint bubblegum. I share it with Emma, but she
prefers to leave it to me. Ever since she almost died, I love her even
more.

Mommy is late, Mima makes us pasta with zucchini, I help her
to grate the parmesan, she tells me about her granny who taught
her all her recipes, she was Italian, she called her Nonna.

Mommy is really late, I'm worried, maybe she had an accident. I
can hear my heart starting to make a noise again, but then she rings
at the gate. I dive on her, Emma does, too, we have a long hug, she
smells of patchouli and cigarettes, it stinks, I'll never smoke.

Mima says it's late, we should sleep here, Mommy says okay,
and the three of us sleep together in Daddy's room.

6:12 P.M.

I can see on Agathe's face how much she'd like to take off and how much effort she's making to stay. I try explaining several times that we have to go, but the Garcias seem too pleased to have us there to let us leave, and the well-being of others always trumps what I want. That may seem like a quality, but when I find myself tipping the hairdresser to thank him for making me look like a toilet brush, or going along with a colleague saying stuff that's borderline racist, it becomes a liability. I've long claimed that it's my excessive empathy that makes me avoid putting people into awkward situations, but I think, in reality, the reason is much more trivial—it's about my desire to be loved.

Agathe holds her phone to her ear:

"Hello? No . . . Really? Of course, I'll be there right away!" (She ends the call, looking horrified.) "I'm so sorry, I have to go, my friend Laura has just had an accident, she's in hospital, apparently it's very serious."

She combines speaking with moving and leaves the kitchen, goes through the corridor, the garden, while I follow her, followed in turn by Madame Garcia.

"Come back whenever you like!" she says to me as I go through the gate. "I hope her friend will get better . . . And about the cat, check with the owner of No. 14. I believe your grandmother and he were very good friends."

Even her conspiratorial air doesn't succeed in shaking my politeness. I thank her for her welcome, and return to Mima's. Agathe is helping herself to a handful of peanuts in the kitchen.

"Don't know what made me want to puke more," she says, grimacing. "Their orange juice or their son."

"Want me to drive you to the hospital?"

"Course not!" she says, amused. "I didn't think I was that good an actress."

"It did occur to me that I haven't heard of any Laura."

"She doesn't exist, I didn't want to jinx one of my real friends by pretending they'd had an accident. I'm really sorry, I didn't mean to scare you, but I couldn't remain in his presence a minute longer."

I take my own handful of peanuts:

"He was a kid, he must have changed."

"Impossible, he's incurable. Prick-in-brain, stage IV, inoperable."

I can't help but laugh, and Agathe, despite trying to maintain her scowl, creases up, too. We pour ourselves some wine and settle down on cushions scattered on the grass, in the shade of the linden tree. Thanks to the position of the house on the hills above Anglet, you can see, in the distance, over the red roofs and gardens, the imposing silhouettes of the Pyrenees.

"Are you seeing someone at the moment?" I ask Agathe.

She shakes her head.

"Not anymore, as of three weeks ago."

I don't have to push her to tell me her story with Mathieu. He was a speech therapist at the nursing home she works at. For once, she stresses, she hadn't fallen madly in love with him the first second, and hadn't been ready to marry him the second second.

"For months, we were friends. We got on really well, had the same sense of humor."

"Oh no . . . "

"We'd go to the movies, go skiing, binge watch TV together," Agathe continues, not reacting to my teasing.

She plunges right back into the relationship while telling me about it. For Christmas they'd gone to London. She'd long dreamt of seeing the festive decorations and lights. As they emerged from the Channel tunnel she kissed him for the first time, an expression of her joy at coming out alive. I interrupt her to congratulate her—there was a time when she was incapable of using an elevator—she thanks me and continues. Mathieu soon moved in with her. She was waiting for the moment she'd start to tire of him, not be able to stand him anymore, that's how all her relationships had gone up until then, but this time it was different.

"He was the one, I'm sure of it. Maybe precisely because he'd been my friend before being my guy."

"What happened?"

She takes a long time to stub out her cigarette.

"He couldn't take it, you know, my . . . my . . . well, me."

She gathers her hair into a topknot, playing it cool, but I see how much she's struggling not to break down.

"You're sure that's why?" I ask.

"Certain. He told me it was too much of a daily strain. I don't blame him, sometimes I think that if I could dump myself, I would."

I search for the words to comfort her, but she doesn't allow me time. Changing the subject seems the best option, to her.

"And you, Alex? How long has it been now?"

"Nineteen years. And still standing."

"And all's well between the two of you?"

"It's fine, I can't complain."

She stares at me, wide-eyed:

"It's enviable! A real advertisement for life as a couple."

I laugh, acknowledging my lack of enthusiasm, and explain it to her.

There's no thrill anymore. Stealthily, passion has slipped away in favor of a deeper feeling that's more comfortable but also far less exciting. I think back to our early days, to those butterflies in the tummy, those palpitations, our heads in the clouds, it was all that mattered, it pushed everything else aside and made us invincible. For a time, I found it hard to accept that I'd never feel that way again.

"You know, it never lasts," Agathe says. "Personally, I dream of that: staying together long enough to build real bonds. Knowing the other person well enough to entrust my life to him. Knowing how he'll react in advance. No bad surprises. Understanding each other with a single glance. Having shared memories. Being loved for who I am, not for who I seem to be. The problem is that I tire of it as soon as it starts to just tick along nicely. I dream of having something that I can't bear."

Clusters of clouds drift over the mountains. I lay my hand on her shoulder.

"You'll find someone who loves you as you are, Agathe. He was just an idiot. There's no reason for anyone to leave you."

She remains silent for a moment, then, without looking at me, replies:

"And yet that's what you did."

I'm fourteen today. Agathe was nine yesterday. At first, I couldn't bear her being born the day before my birthday, but now I like it because we get to spend an evening at the restaurant, the two of us with Mom.

It's rare, the three of us being together. Mom works a lot, and on Friday evening she goes out with her friends, so I watch over Agathe and we eat cereal while watching The X-Files and Tales from the Crypt. They're scary, so afterwards, we jump as soon as a door slams in the building, and that makes us laugh. We don't tell Mom about it because she'd forbid us from watching because of Agathe's anxiety.

Every year we go to the same restaurant. I was allowed to wear mascara, specially.

Mom gives me a Nirvana T-shirt, I'm pleased but sad, because Kurt Cobain died last week. Agathe gets a Dance Machine CD, and screams with delight—East 17 and Corona are both on it—I suspect she's going to do our ears in, and she already listens non-stop to Ace of Base . . .

Mom tells us about the day we were born, like she does every year. We laugh when she says I sulked when I first saw Agathe. Just after, she went off in an incubator because of her lungs, and apparently I was pleased. I don't remember that, but I've changed my opinion. She's not bad, as a sister, and also, she's the only person I can talk about Dad with.

I order a burger and fries, which we don't get to eat often, but Mom makes me have green beans instead of fries. There are two people at the next table, Thomas and his father. He sees me but *ignores me. It lasted a week, between the two of us. He broke it off because I had fake Doc Martens, as my mother couldn't afford real ones. Shortly after, he went out with Julie-the-slut, who's got a Chappy bike and a Chevignon bag.*

With dessert, we get the same surprise from Mom as every year. It comes with candles, all the wait staff sing "Happy Birthday," and my mother does, too. I just want the ground to open up and swallow me. Thomas watches me, I can see very well he's just laughing at me. I'm so ashamed.

Mom's in a bad mood for the entire journey home. She says I'm ungrateful, that I could have smiled, said thank you. I try to apologize, but she's having none of it. She slams the door as we go into the apartment. Agathe takes my defense, saying I was embarrassed because of Thomas, but Mom explodes, screams, hits the wall, we freeze, but it's not enough, she's too wound up. I know what's coming to us as soon she takes the belt off her jeans. She wraps the buckle around her hand and moves towards Agathe. It's the first time I don't let her do it. I grab my sister by the hand and drag her into my room, then lock the door. Mom bangs on the door. We sit on the bed, Agathe curls into me. I hold her in my arms.

It finally stops.

Mom has calmed down.

Agathe laughs at the sight of me. I've got mascara all down my cheeks.

I get up, look at the calendar hanging on the wall. I count the squares separating us from the summer vacation at Mima's. There are eighty-nine nights to go before the good times.

I t's soon Christmas.
Last year, I'd made things out of salt dough for everyone. A
heart for Mommy, a flower for Mima, a fish for Papi, a snow-
man for Jérôme, a rugby ball for Laurent, a moon for uncle, and
a ladybird for auntie. I'd also made a dog for Daddy, a bit like
Snoopy, although he's curly-haired really, but I forgot to take it on
the day we went to the cemetery, so I put it away in the drawer of
my bedside table.

I love giving presents. I don't put them under the tree, I hand
them out, one by one, that way I can see if they're pleased.

This year, I'm going to paint some lovely pictures, Mommy has
bought me some Canson paper, and they'll be able to hang them
on the wall. It'll be easier for mailing, seeing as we're not spending Christmas with them. It's because of Mommy's new boyfriend,
he doesn't want to know Mima and Papi because they're Daddy's
parents. He's nice, but I preferred Patrick (not the last one, the one
before that). And I don't really know where to look when he speaks
to me because he's got squinty eyes.

Mommy seems happy since he's been living at ours, Emma says
that's the main thing, though it's obvious to me that she can't stand
him, especially when he hogs the bathroom in the morning and
listens to blaring music while she's doing her homework. Maybe
that's why she goes to the gym every evening.

As for me, I've stopped doing judo. I liked it at first, but then I
didn't fancy going anymore. I think the instructor was color-blind,
he must have taken us for black belts, last time I didn't understand
any of it, and at the end of the session, I saw stars and collapsed.

Mommy didn't want me to stop, she said I'd already pulled that one with dance and swimming, but in the end, it suited her not to have to take me to judo.

Next year I'll do drawing, or maybe drama. Actually, no. I'd enjoy the acting, but I couldn't speak in front of loads of people. I've got time to think about it. First I have to finish fourth grade, and then, more importantly, it's summer break. I hope we'll be allowed to go to Mima's, maybe Mommy will have a new boyfriend and he won't be jealous of Daddy.

7:22 A.M.

The sea is even calmer than yesterday. I can relax in it without the risk of being tossed out by a wave while doing my favorite thing: floating like a log. It's only then, facing the sky, rocked by the swell of the water, arms and legs totally limp, that I feel entirely serene. There are still some scattered clouds left over from last night's rain, together with that earthy smell you get after a downpour. I learned recently that it's got a name: petrichor. It refers specifically to that scent that rises from wet soil after a dry period. While looking into it, I discovered that languages of all kinds abound in terms that are little-known, yet so poetic. Thus, in Italian, *umarells* are those elderly men whose pastime is watching building sites, hands clasped behind backs, always ready to offer advice or an opinion. In Japan, the sunlight that filters through the leaves of trees is called *komorebi*. In Portugal, *saudade* is a melancholic feeling that's a mix of nostalgia and hope. I devoted a lesson to this, which my pupils really enjoyed. One of them asked me if there was a word to describe the smell that comes out of the principal's mouth, which his classmates found highly amusing—as did I, though I made sure not to show it.

The cries of seagulls pierce the silence. I return to a vertical position, the old man is at the edge of the water, surrounded by birds. Like yesterday, he plunges his hand into his bag and throws food to them. Further along, a father and child watch the spectacle. I swim a few strokes before coming out. I intend to return to the house with breakfast, I want to be there before Agathe wakes up, even if that's likely to be late, considering what time she got to

bed. We prolonged our evening under the linden tree, made ourselves tomato and mozzarella on bread and had an impromptu
picnic, just as Mima often did. We found the rug she'd use, and
we just stayed there, talking about our lives now, going down
memory lane, until darkness eclipsed daylight. I then went back
to my room and into the arms that Morpheus had been holding
out to me for some time. The wind had risen, heralding rain, but
Agathe remained outside. In the dead of night, I was awoken by
a downpour against the window. Through the curtain, I made out
Agathe, standing in the middle of the garden, her face looking up
at the sky. Thinking she was having a turn, I tore down the stairs
four at a time and ran up to her, but no, she was just fine.

"I love the rain," she said. "Can't see why it's got such a bad
reputation."

She has always liked what others reject, a kind of heightened
Good Samaritan syndrome. She's crazy about Brussels sprouts,
passionate about sharks, and has always been drawn to people
who've been sidelined. One day she adopted a dog, no doubt to
repair the trauma surrounding Snoopy, and, of course, she chose
the ugliest and oldest mutt at the shelter.

"Stay with me," she said, as I was heading back for cover.

I went inside and watched her through the window. She
looked happy. I got a lump in my throat, it's what happens when
expectations and reality match perfectly. By suggesting to my sister that we spend this week together, I knew what I was coming
to do. But my expectation, I realize, lay elsewhere, I just wanted
to reassure myself that she was fine. She was always better than
me at catching happiness as it's flying past. I grabbed an umbrella
from the hall cupboard and returned to her.

"Are you kidding?" she guffawed. "Get rid of that thing,
there's no point otherwise. It's like eating chocolate with an anes-
thetized mouth."

I closed the umbrella and let the water fall into my short hair,
slide down my forehead, my neck.

"Lift your head!" Agathe said.

I closed my eyes and turned my face up to the sky. My T-shirt was drenched, the rain was warm thanks to the summer it was taunting; it ran over my eyelids, my cheeks, my lips, I felt a sob forming in my stomach, rising up to my throat, and escaping into the downpour.

The air is fresher than yesterday, I shiver as I get out of the sea.

"Good morning, monsieur!" I call out to the gulls' friend.

"Go fuck yourself!" he replies, charmingly.

I got a warning. It's the first time that's happened to me, I'm more used to being highly commended. The teachers reckon I've stopped making any effort, and say they want to shock me into knuckling down again. What a rotten idea—if being shot in the foot was motivating, everyone would have a limp. I was even called to the principal's office, she wanted to know what was going on, since I've always been a good pupil. My mother was in the office, she took my defense, explained that things were a bit complicated at home, promised I'd make more of an effort. I promised, too, hoping I'm better at keeping promises made to others than to myself, which I make every evening, then break every morning.

Stéphanie, Marion and Nicolas were waiting for me in the corridor to go back to class. Since I've been hanging out with them, Margaux's stopped talking to me. She says I've changed. She's jealous, I've never had so many friends since I stopped being the crawler in the front row. They invited me to the party at Arnaud's on Saturday afternoon, I'd really like to go.

Mom is parked outside the school. I find that weird, I normally get the bus, but she takes me to have a drink at a bar near the church. As soon as we're seated, she asks me if I'm angry with her.

I reply with the truth, that sometimes I'm angry, sometimes sad, sometimes scared. She starts to cry, so I add that most often, I'm happy. She says she's a terrible mother. She explains that she hates herself, and that's why she drinks. That Dad's death didn't help matters. That the more she wants to stop, the more she drinks, because she realizes that she's not managing to, and she needs to forget that she's useless. She tells me that, often, she can feel the rage in her stomach, like a monster taking over, that her mother was the same, that she's done everything not to be like her, but it's stronger than her, she can't control it. She strokes my hair, kisses me, repeatedly. She's concerned about my grades, she thought we were doing fine. She keeps asking me if I love her. If she knew how much. If she knew that, every morning, I go to check she's breathing. If she knew that I speak to no one about all this so no one can think badly of her. If she knew that, every time I have to make a wish, I wish for her and my sister to be happy. If she knew that the reason I'm in such a hurry to grow up is to be able to help her. I tell her that I love her very much, and hold nothing against her.

"You're more mature than I am," she says.

She orders a second coffee and announces to me that she's going away for five weeks. She's going to alcohol rehab, and getting help for her depression. I ask her if there isn't some other solution, but apparently not. Mima will come and look after us, it's all been arranged. I can't seem to swallow my cola anymore.

We go to collect Agathe from school. She usually gets the bus, too. She's worried when she sees us, thinks something serious must have happened. Mom reassures her, we stop off at the bakery, and go home. There are two suitcases in the hall. I hadn't realized it would happen so fast. My throat is burning, I hold back my tears, Agathe mustn't understand. Mom explains to her that she's going to Brittany for a while, for work. Agathe asks loads of questions, and she believes the answers. I'm jealous: I wish I could believe them, too.

Mom suggests we sleep with her for her last night at home, her in the middle, my sister and me on either side. I soon find myself in the cold, without a comforter, with my mother's elbow stuck in my back, but I really don't care, we're all together.

From tomorrow onwards, it's a promise, I'll work hard. Never mind about Saturday afternoon.

M ima woke us up really early to go to the Rhune. Apparently, it's a mountain from which you can see all of the Basque Country. I'd have liked to sleep some more, so I do in the car, but, after a while, I have to look at the road because the bends are bringing my breakfast back up.

Papi puts on his cassette of Basque songs and sings along in a gruff voice to make us laugh.

There's already a crowd when we arrive, we queue a little, and then get onto a train all made of wood. There's no glass in the windows. Mima lets us sit beside the opening, telling us we'll have the loveliest view. Papi is behind his camcorder, filming the landscape.

On our bench there's a lady with her two daughters, it makes me think of Mommy. I wish she was with us. She stayed in Brittany longer than planned, she sent us letters and sometimes phoned us. When she got back, all three of us slept together for a week. She promised us she'd never go away again.

While the train goes up, I take photos with the disposable camera. It's really pretty, we pass some ponies, Mima explains to us that they're called Pottoks.

When we reach the top, it's a bit cold, but luckily Mima brought some jackets. I don't know why, it makes me want to give her a big hug, so I throw myself into her arms, which makes her laugh. A few people are already there, apparently they walked up (they're crazy!) (or maybe they didn't know about the train).

I've never seen anything so beautiful. On the right, you can see the whole coast, the sea in the distance, the Basque Country inland. Emma and I look through Mima's binoculars and try to recognize the villages. We can see Ciboure, Saint-Jean-de-Luz, Bidart, Ascain, Nivelle, we even manage to spot the Rock of the Virgin in Biarritz. It looks minuscule, like a land for dolls!

On the left you can see the Pyrenees, and, below us, white clouds that approach like the waves of the sea. I take loads of photos, it's magnificent, and at one moment I realize that tears are running down my cheeks, but I don't know if it's the wind or the beauty. Papi films me, so I hide under my jacket.

We're going to walk around a bit, not too much because it's steep for Mima, we see a shepherd calling his flock, we see some more Pottoks, but don't go near so as not to frighten them, and then we go into the restaurant and I drink the best hot chocolate I've ever drunk, but I don't say that to Mima so as not to offend her.

In the end, I'm really pleased not to have slept on. I think that, when I'm grown up, I'd like to live in the Basque Country. I'll just have to convince Mommy and Emma, because I won't leave without them.

11:06 A.M.

I've always loved going into the garage. It was Papi's den. He'd spend time in it tinkering around, painting, imagining all the new things he could make. He was particularly proud of the wooden worktable in which Mima kept all her sewing gear; the barrel he turned into a bar that lit up when you opened the door; and the revolving shelf he installed in the kitchen.

Nothing has moved. His fishing rods are leaning against the wall, beside the cool box. There's still that smell of paint. The tools are hanging on the wall, above the workbench. As if he'd just left the garage.

"Found one?" Emma asks, joining me.

"Not yet," I say, opening a drawer.

We're looking for a lightbulb—the one in the kitchen is spent. Papi had a whole stock of them, like he did pens, batteries, power strips. He never spoke about his childhood, but Mima had told us, one day, that his parents had been killed during the war and he'd been brought up by his very strict grandparents. I'd inferred that he'd been deprived of everything, and his hoarding was to make up for it.

Opening another drawer, I happen upon a little piece of my childhood.

A small recorder and some cassettes. My heart contracts.

1991, maybe 1992. It was summer. The previous night, while stargazing, Emma spotted a strange shape in the sky. I asked if it could be a flying saucer. Mima laughed and said there's no such thing. Emma and I weren't so sure. We preferred to think that extraterrestrials were nice and had come to make contact with us. All night long, our imaginations were in overdrive. The following morning, still sleepy-eyed, we joined Papi at the table in the sitting room, where he'd been waiting for us.

"Girls, I have something for you."

He pushed forward a recorder and pressed the play button. Suddenly, strange, dissonant sounds, then a voice rose up, nasal, almost tinny. We discovered an extraordinary language, never heard until then. I can still see Emma's eyes, round as marbles, and mine can't have been less so. We were astounded.

"Do you think they're extraterrestrials?" I asked.

Papi nodded his head:

"Absolutely. The cassette was placed outside the front door. By chance, I have a friend who works at a space agency. He was able to translate the message, on condition that we never speak about it to anyone. Do you promise?"

"We promise, Papi!" we replied in unison.

He took a piece of paper out of his pocket and unfolded it, then cleared his throat, to indicate to us that it was a solemn moment.

"Message to Emma and Agathe Delorme. We've observed you from our distant galaxy, and we came to Earth to tell you that you are two extraordinary little girls. You're the pride and joy of your loved ones. Well done!"

I kept the secret, and I'm sure Emma did, too. We never spoke of it again, firstly out of fear of extraterrestrial reprisals, then, as the years went by, fear of spoiling the magic of the scene. Certain childhood memories are like very old paintings, they spoil when exposed to light. So we keep them somewhere inside of us, hidden from view, intact.

I hold the little recorder in my hands and a wave of emotion overwhelms me. In the half-light of his garage, I can imagine

Papi inventing the gibberish, holding his nose and hitting metal objects to add the sound effects, just so his two granddaughters would feel unique in the world.

"I've found a bulb!"

I join Emma, we leave the garage, and close up Papi's cave once more.

1:01 P.M.

"Could you come and empty the dishwasher?"

I'm looking at my phone while waiting for the potatoes to cook. I've laid the table and chopped tomatoes and onions, but Emma has clearly decided to put an end to the relationship between the chair and my ass. I get up with all the enthusiasm of a slug and join her in the kitchen.

"I presume I shouldn't put any ham in the salad?" she asks, while making the vinaigrette.

"You can put it in, but I won't eat it."

"It doesn't bother you if it touches your food?"

"Is that a real question, or are you making fun of me?"

She doesn't reply. I put away the glasses, the plates, I can see her watching me out of the corner of her eye, I get to the cutlery—forks, spoons, knives . . .

"By the way, just so you know, the blades go down."

I stop what I'm doing and look at her:

"Meaning?"

"The knives. Last night you didn't put them in blade down in the basket, you can cut yourself taking them out."

"You just have to take care. Blade down, they're not properly washed."

"Of course they are. And also, the cutlery needs to be sorted. Knives in one basket, forks in another, and so on."

She speaks while stirring the vinaigrette, looking deep into the bowl.

"Emma, you have your way, I have mine."

"Mine's more logical."

"More tight-assed, for sure."

She stops stirring.

"What's your problem?" she asks.

"Are you serious? I have the problem? You've been on my back since earlier, I'm just reacting."

She lets out an exaggerated laugh:

"Of course, it was pain-in-the-ass Emma who started it! Agathe's far too cool to stir things up!"

"Have you lost the plot, or what? Emma, stop, you're really driving me crazy."

"So? What are you going to do about it? Slam the door, insult me, have a fit? As usual? You're great at spoiling the party, I'd forgotten."

A ball of anger is forming in my stomach. I could almost hold it in my hands, it's compact, heavy, oppressive. My entire body is shaking, my breathing quickening. The words are jostling in my head, I'm struggling not to hurl them right at her. I chuck the knives into the drawer and shut myself in my room before I say anything I'll regret.

2:05 P.M.

"Agathe?"

It's the third time in an hour that she's come knocking on my door. I've locked it. I don't answer. She can just fuck off.

3:12 P.M.

"Agathe, you must eat something."

"Get lost."

"Your food's ready. I'm waiting for you, to eat mine."

" . . . "

"I didn't put in any ham."

" . . . "

"I've poured you some cola."

These are apologies in disguise.

My anger has simmered down. We've wasted enough time. I open the door, she's standing there, smiling awkwardly.

"You know what they say, Gagathe, about tough love."

"Yeah, well any more 'tough love' from you and it's not the knife blades that'll be upside-down."

The school nurse said it would be good if I went and saw a shrink. When I told Mommy, she said no way, shrinks are for crazy people. Emma said that's mainly because Mom's scared I'll tell the shrink uncomfortable things.

I wish I could manage to get to sleep at night. Every time I go to bed, it's the same old thing, I think about death, my own, Emma's, Mommy's, Mima's, Papi's, and my heart beats too fast for me to sleep. I'm scared of fires, too. There was one in the building next door, Christmas evening. We were at Mima's, so we didn't see it, but when we got back, the outside wall was all black and the balcony had gotten burnt. Apparently, it was the Christmas tree that caught fire. Emma says that's rare, that there's no reason that will happen to ours. Every evening since I've had this fear, she helps me check that all the radiators in the apartment are uncovered and the gas properly turned off. Then she comes to my room and answers all my questions until my heart calms down. If it starts racing again, I can go and sleep with her, in her bed. Mommy doesn't want to hear a word about my anxieties. She says I'm putting it on to get the attention. She's probably right, but I don't know why I do that.

I preferred it when I was younger, I had fewer nagging questions in my head. And I preferred elementary school, too. I had my friends. Céline is in one sixth-grade class and I'm in another. We see each other at recess, but the rest of the time I'm all alone. It's nice of her to stick with me all the same, despite the others giving me a hard time. They could lay into her, too. I don't know why they're like that to me. It's mainly Noémie and Julia, two fifth-grade girls. They decided I'd looked at them the wrong way, and ever since, they steal my afternoon snack and mock me in the schoolyard, because of my big nose.

Céline advised me to tell my mother about it, but it'll worry her, so I'd rather not.

This morning, it was back to school after the All Saints' Day break, and I didn't feel like going at all. I made out I had a stomachache, which I get every month since my periods came, but Mommy didn't want to hear about it, and I had to take the bus. It was okay in the end, the girls just cut off a strand of my hair. Could've been worse.

Emma is waiting for me outside the school gate. My heart immediately starts racing. It's not normal, something must have happened. She pecks me on the cheek and tells me to point out Noémie and Julia to her. I ask her how she knows, and just then Céline turns up. I have no choice, I point out the two girls as they're leaving, my sister heads off in their direction, and I'm just left there, scared it's going to end badly. I don't hear what she says to them, she seems calm, Noémie buries her nose in her scarf, Julia nods her head, and that's it, off they go and Emma returns to me and tells me that it's all sorted, that they'll never trouble me again.

I hate my sister. I wish she'd never been born. My whole life is dedicated to looking out for her. I played with Barbie until I was fifteen just to keep her occupied, I spend my nights reassuring her, I stick her in front of a cartoon show so she doesn't see Mom's meltdowns, I help her with her homework, and despite all that, she manages to ruin my life.

She didn't do it on purpose, but still. Without her, it wouldn't have happened.

It all started when I slept with Arnaud. I'd intended to wait, to be sure he was the right one, but he told me he didn't want a girl, he needed a real woman, and if I didn't want to, he was leaving me. It was really painful, I bit the inside of my cheeks so as not to cry out. After a month, he told me I must go on the Pill because he can't stand condoms. I told him I didn't really agree to it, because of AIDS, and all that, but apparently he's had a test and he hasn't got it. Obviously, there's no way I can talk to Mom about this, so I went to the family planning center. Margaux came with me, we've been talking again for a while now. The lady was nice, and explained everything to me clearly, but I had to lie to her, because she insisted we use condoms all the same. She prescribed me a pill, I went to collect it at the pharmacy, and I hid the box in my koala backpack, on top of the wardrobe in my room. No one's touched it for years, so little chance of that happening. I wrote a "P" in felt pen on the light switch in my room, so I remember to take it every evening when going to bed.

After school, I hung out in the park with Stéphanie, we'd brought along some magazines, we read them. In Star Club, there were two pages on G-Squad, and I love them, especially Gérald, but I don't tell anyone, it's cooler to listen to Nirvana. Cindy Crawford was on the cover of Jeune et Jolie, she's beautiful, I'd like to look like her. Life must be easier when you're beautiful.

My mother was in the kitchen, making supper, when I got home. She said hello normally, I wasn't expecting what was to come. On the coffee table in the sitting room, I saw my koala bag, open, and my started pack of pills sticking out of it. I felt the blood rush straight to my head. I went to my room to do my homework, dreading my mother turning up at any moment, but nothing. At supper she seemed normal, even laughed several times. It was weird. I knew I had to talk to her about it, so I waited until dessert. I'd been preparing my speech in my head the whole evening, but all I managed to say was, "Why did you poke around in my things?".

It was the biggest hiding of my life. She grabbed me by the hair and kept hitting me, for several minutes. Agathe was crying, with her hands over her ears.

Later, Mom came to my room to talk to me, to tell me that she didn't like having to do that, but it was for my own good. She kissed me on the cheek, where a bruise was coming up. Agathe checked she'd turned in before coming to slide into my bed. She said sorry, it was her who'd found my pills, she'd wanted to play with my bag. She thought it was medicine, that I was sick, she was scared, so she told Mom about it. I threw her out. I hate her. The day I'm eighteen, I'll be off.

5:54 P.M.

"It's a stargazing night," Agathe said to me.

"I'll go get the telescope," I replied.

We packed a bag, had a bite to eat, and hit the road, having plastered a few "missing" posters for Robert Redford around the neighborhood, and rang the doorbell of the neighbor at no. 14, in vain.

It's a tradition. Mima would take us every year. At the beginning of August, over several nights, there are showers of shooting stars. To see them most clearly, it's best to be far from the light pollution of towns. Our little spot is in Itxassou, the village our grandmother grew up in. When I was little, I dreamed of the city and its hustle and bustle. I always wanted to see lots of people, to move, feel like I was making something of life, rather than the opposite. And yet here, from the very first time, surrounded by green hills, with the mountains as our horizon, in this village stuck right in the middle of the Basque hinterland, I felt the greatest serenity. As if nothing could happen to me here.

Mima was passionate about astronomy. She initiated us both very early on. On the table in the sitting room, covered with its indestructible yellow waxed cloth, she'd open big illustrated books, their pages giving off that familiar old-paper smell. And then she could talk to us for hours about planets, constellations, galaxies, and for hours, we hung on her every word. She had a gift for making any subject fascinating. I'm pretty sure I'd have been hooked on the history of cloves in interwar France if she'd told it to me. Regularly, when a night was favorable for observation, she'd drag her old telescope into the garden and point it up at the sky, make a few adjustments, and invite us to press our expectant peepers to the eyepiece. And then we'd discover Saturn, the Moon, Venus, Jupiter, oohing and aahing all the while.

We drive into the village. Since setting off, we've been listening to the soundtrack of our past, and the playlist is all over the place: we move shamelessly from Ophélie Winter to No Doubt, from Ménélik to Britney Spears, from The Offspring to Lara Fabian.

"You can park in the lot before the Pas de Roland," Agathe tells me, lowering the volume.

"Okay."

The road leads us past the house Mima grew up in. She'd become all nostalgic every time she saw it. She'd point out any changes, the recently repainted wall, the new swing, the oak having been pruned. In this garden, insignificant to passers-by, her memories would dance.

She'd skip from one to another, we'd listen distractedly, not realizing their importance. For us, they were words, abstract images; for her, they were a part of her life still attached to the present. I understand it now. When you recount a memory you see it, hear it, even feel it. You relive it, entirely. But the person listening can just try to visualize it, and even then, only if they're empathetic or the subject interests them. Otherwise, they wait patiently for the end of the anecdote to tell one of their own or move on to another subject.

Mima would tell of her father who'd take her to the farm, her mother who taught her to knit beside the fire, her grandmother who spoke only Italian, and, especially, her beloved little brother. He featured in all her memories. Until the day she died, he remained her dearest friend. He had left to live outside of Marseille, but ritually, every Sunday evening, to ward off the blues, they'd phone each other.

At the last moment, impulsively, I leave the road leading to the Pas de Roland and drive towards the village. From the corner of my eye, I see Agathe smiling.

6:06 P.M.

It's not the first time I've climbed over the low stone wall of the Itxassou cemetery. Mima's parents are buried here, she brought us several times. She would clean up the grave and replace the sole pot plant, its only ornamentation. The fragile, vulnerable Mima only ever appeared in this isolated little cemetery, as if the place took her on a journey into the past, and she returned, momentarily, to being the young orphan she'd once been.

Papi was buried here, too. Mima now lies beside him. It's at Itxassou that their story had begun, at Itxassou that they'd decided it should end.

"Take your time!" Agathe calls out, stopping at the entrance.

"You're not coming?"

"You've got things to talk about, together."

The grave is covered in bouquets of mostly wilted flowers. I throw them into the trash can and clean the plaques. I feel nothing. I try my hardest to make tears come, I summon up happy memories, I read the name of my adored grandmother on the stone, I even find myself grimacing to get the lacrimal glands going—they say that appetite comes with eating, so maybe grief comes with crying—but nothing works.

For several long minutes, I stare, impassively, at my grandmother's tomb. Agathe ends up joining me. She puts her arm around my waist and rests her head on my shoulder.

"We're lucky to have each other."

I tilt my head and rest it gently on hers.

I don't know how I'd have got through all this without my sister. I realize how lucky I am not to be alone in bearing my sorrows. How lucky not to be alone in seeing, hearing and sensing my lost ones. How lucky to have a head on which to rest my own.

We stay there for a while; the heat is oppressive. Aside from the odd hum of a motor, silence reigns over Itxassou. Shutters are closed, they'll be reopened later, when it's cooler.

"Shall we go?" Agathe asks.

"I can't manage to cry."

She looks at me, her cheeks streaming with tears.

"It doesn't matter. You've always cried internally."

We leave the cemetery, but not before I turn one last time towards the grave. Then I take my sister's hand and we go on our way.

7:14 P.M.

The Pas de Roland is situated in a gorge created by the river Nive. It's a rock with a passageway carved through it, and every year, Mima would tell us the legend surrounding it. Roland, the son of Charlemagne, was being pursued by enemy troops and a rock barred his way, so, without further ado, he cut through it with his sword. We walk along the river to reach it, loaded with two full knapsacks and the telescope. We pass through it to get to the little beach a few meters beyond and sit down in the shade. It's the route Mima always made us take. We discovered much later that we could get there by car. But the magic's not the same when the journey is not brimming with the past.

"Shall we have a dip?" Agathe suggests.

The fresh water tumbles onto the rocks, and I don't need to dip a toe in to know it's freezing cold.

"Out of the question."

"Well, I'm going in!" she cries, jumping up.

She takes off her sandals and dress, and is left in her underwear. I check that no one can see us. A legacy from my mother. Not drawing attention to yourself, ensuring you don't bother anyone. If invisibility could be bought in a store, she'd have gifted it to us at birth. But it can't, so Agathe runs to the river, swearing at the pebbles hurting her feet along the way.

I really didn't want to go to London with my class, didn't want to go so far away from my mother and sister, but in the end, it's great. Mélanie and I got a nice family, except they eat this jelly that's gross, and even more gross, vinegar-flavored chips. And Mélanie and I had never spoken before—the whole class makes fun of her, a bit like they do me, but with her, it's because she stutters. Personally, it doesn't bother me, and anyhow, even if she does speak to me strangely, at least she speaks to me, which isn't true of everyone.

I was sure that, being far from home, I'd have anxiety attacks, but, apart from on the ferry when I thought we were going to sink, everything's fine.

We watched the Changing of the Guard at Buckingham Palace (boring), visited the Museum of London (boring), walked around Westminster (not bad), and best of all, we had free time to go shopping (brilliant). Mom gave me a little pocket money, Mima sent me some, and my sister cracked open her piggy bank to give me a banknote. I don't really get the prices, not being in francs, but everything seems mega expensive. I've still got enough money to bring presents back for everyone. For my Mom, I got a pen with a red double-decker bus that moves inside it; for Mima, a notebook with Queen Elizabeth on the cover; and best of all, for Emma, I got a file full of postcards of the Spice Girls. She's going to be pleased, she loves them!

It's our last evening. I'm starting to miss my family and can't wait to go home tomorrow. We play hide-and-seek with the English family's two little boys. They're funny, they look at us as if we're from another planet and ask us loads of questions. The older one asked me if we had electricity in France. I explained that we didn't, and no water, either, so we washed in the river with the fish.

After that we chatted a bit with the parents, but I don't understand everything because me and English don't get on, so I say "yes" to everything, nodding my head and smiling, like those dogs at the back of cars. And that's how I ended up with a second helping of that gross jelly.

When we go off to bed, Mélanie opens the room's small window and takes out a pack of cigarettes. She offers me one, but I tell her that we're not allowed to, that they'll smell it, that we'll get into trouble. She doesn't care, just sits on the windowsill and coolly smokes. The mother arrives, and calmly asks her to put it out. I don't know where to put myself, just want to disappear, and my heart is pounding in my ears. Mélanie stubs out the cigarette and shuts the window.

Tomorrow, the teachers will punish us, for sure. They'll tell Mom about it. She'll be disappointed in me. Everything gets all mixed up in my tummy. I don't know if I'm sad, angry, or anxious. I go out of the room and lock myself in the bathroom. I know what to do to calm myself down. I've done it for a while now, it works well. I grab the compass in my pocket, pull my trousers down, and scratch the skin of my thigh with the sharp point.

W e were supposed to spend Christmas at Mima's and Papi's, but Uncle J-Y spoilt everything. He took them to Spain for the holidays, without us.
I counted the days for nothing.
I hate the lot of them.

11:43 P.M.

It's magnificent. Sublime. Extraordinary. There aren't enough words.

When I was little, I'd wait for stargazing night with almost unbearable impatience. I used to wait for nearly everything with unbearable impatience. Everything seemed better to me than the present. The present was only good for waiting, regretting, it was a kind of bridge between yesterday and tomorrow, between the past and the future, between nostalgia and impatience. Before I'd even reached the moment so longed for, before I'd even lived it, I was already overcome with irrepressible melancholy. I tried to remedy this, throwing myself into meditation, plowing through books on personal growth, but although I learned to see the waiting as a prologue to the much-anticipated moment, the day that follows still gives me a hangover.

Every summer, then, I'd wait impatiently for stargazing night. It was the promise of hours shared with Mima, but also of a dazzling spectacle: the ballet of those shooting stars. Mima would bring us here, first to the Pas de Roland to cool down and have a bite to eat, then to the top of one of Itxassou's hills, far from the light pollution, where she'd set up her telescope. We'd peer at planets, nebulae, and galaxies, before stretching out on the ground. I'd always make the same wish when a star tore through the sky. In my head, so it wouldn't lose its power: "I wish for my sister, grandmother, and mother to be happy all their lives."

Later, at the age when lucidity starts to darken the sky of childhood, anxiety crept into proceedings. I'd picture myself, minuscule, insignificant, beneath all this vastness. These stars, most having disappeared long before, would just remind me of our transience. In my mid-teens, I gave up the tradition, and, despite myself, ended my grandmother's pleasure in passing her passion on to us. Three or four years ago, I went to Mima's one August evening and took her to Itxassou. She didn't seem surprised, as if she was expecting me. Once there, despite her trying to be discreet, I found her in tears.

It's always breathtaking, I must stop myself from thinking too much, but the magic works anew.

"Another one!" Emma exclaims, pointing at the sky.

"I don't know who to make wishes for anymore!"

"Make one for me."

"Already have. I wished for you to be reincarnated as a dishwasher so you can throw the upside-down knives into the eyes of whoever put them in that way."

She sits up:

"I know, I am a bit rigid about certain things."

"Girl, only titanium's more rigid than you."

"Come on, you know the knives aren't nearly as well washed, blade up. It's like the plates, if you don't space them out enough, the water can't circulate, it's just logical!"

"I think you even surpass titanium."

She bursts into laughter.

"D'you know who was like that?" she asks.

"Hitler?"

"Duh . . . Dad. When we went to his place, we had to put our shoes perpendicular to the wall, otherwise he'd have to align them himself."

"I don't remember that at all."

A wave of sadness hits me.

"I don't remember much about him, in fact."

"You were only six. I was eleven, so had more time to stock up memories."

"Tell me some."

She pours herself another glass of wine and lies back down, facing the stars:

"He used to drive fast. I remember being scared, especially when he took that bend just before our road. I was convinced that it was right there that I'd die one day. He'd listen to Johnny Hallyday, he knew his songs by heart, he was forever singing '*Que je t'aime*' to Mom."

"Oh yes! I do remember that!"

The image forms in my mind with impressive clarity. I'm sitting at the white melamine-coated table, I can almost feel the cold metal leg against my shin. We've just finished eating, my mother is emptying a plate into the trash can. My plate is still full (I already hated green beans). I must finish them if I want to get down from the table, my father has said. He stands up, puts his arm around my mother, and starts singing: "*Que je t'aime, que je t'aime, que je t'aime!*" My mother rolls her eyes, but he keeps going with even more gusto, and she finally cracks up laughing.

"I remember his leather jacket," I say. "I loved its smell when he'd give me a kiss as he came home from work."

"When he did come home."

"He didn't always come home?"

"No. Mom sometimes waited all night for him. I'd get up several times to see if he was back, she'd still be sitting on the sofa. She'd shout at me, not wanting me to see her crying."

"D'you think he was cheating on her?" I ask.

"I don't know . . . Can't see what else he could've been doing. Hey! Another shooting star!"

I never contemplated my father having bad sides to him. That's the privilege of the dead, they take their flaws to the grave.

This man whom, in the end, I know so little has haunted my every day.

I didn't grow up without a father. I grew up with a dead father. I built my personality on what was missing. His absence marked my identity, like a middle name or a beauty spot. It was one of the first things I'd announce when meeting someone: "My father is dead." It was awkward, especially when that someone was a sales assistant polite enough to greet me in a store or something. At home, we weren't allowed to talk about it. It was a taboo subject, like periods, sex, and football. Once, I tried hanging a photo of him above my bed; it disappeared within a day.

I grew up as the girl who had lost her father. I inspired curiosity, sometimes pity. When Father's Day was approaching, certain conversations would stop when I turned up. It was rare, most of the kids' parents were both very much alive. At a time when the slightest difference put you into a box, I found myself between the gingers and the gays.

It wasn't all drawbacks. Sometimes I used it as an excuse. When behaving badly, or fooling around, I'd pull out my immunity card: "You must understand me, I lost my father."

I even used it to ease my conscience, convinced myself that everything stemmed from it, that my anxieties, my distress, those emotions that made me feel different, were due to this early bereavement. Everyone believed it, it was an untouchable excuse.

I wasn't entirely wrong. My own death was always far too alive in my mind.

"I just felt a drop," Emma says.

"A bird must have peed on you."

I've barely finished my sentence when the rain decides to join us. It doesn't arrive on tiptoe, spitting one drop here, one drop there, oh no. It opens all the floodgates and pours the lot onto our heads: Here you are, it's a present, no need to thank me.

I like the rain, but it mustn't push its luck.

We pack up rug, picnic, and telescope, run to the car, regretting parking so far away after all, jump inside, look at each other, drenched, dripping, beaming.

"The fragrance of happiness is stronger in the rain," Emma says, chuckling.

"I don't think you've ever said anything so dumb."

Emma's taking me to see Titanic. It's her third time seeing it. I wasn't that keen on watching a movie about a boat that sank, with people in period costume, but as everyone's talking about it, I felt like I was missing something mega, and I'm fed up with seeming like a girl who's been left behind.

We brought M&M's and cola from home, they're too expensive at the cinema. My sister is with her boyfriend, Loïc. They've been together for several months, and he seems less of an idiot than Arnaud. I thought she'd never get over it, when that bright spark dumped her for Alexia. She wrote him letters, went and rang at his door, and the rest of the time she was curled up in bed. I'd go and join her every night, to snuggle up, but not because of my own anxiety for once.

We sit in the back row, right in the middle. Loïc says that's where the sound is best. Emma starts to cry at the opening credits. I ask her what's up, she says: "It's because I know Jack's going to die."

I cannot believe it.

I'm about to spend three hours and fourteen minutes stuck in a dark movie theater, right behind a guy with a bird's nest instead of hair, all to see a movie to which my sister has just blurted out the ending. I prefer her buried in her bed, after all.

E mmanuel Petit has just scored the third goal. Loïc jumps into my arms, yelling with joy. France are world champions. We watched the match in his studio, with all his friends.

There are around twenty of us, all daubed and clad in blue, white, and red. I came over just for the final, returning to Mima's tomorrow.

Outside, car horns are heralding the victory and people are starting to pour into the streets. We go down to join the crowd, Loïc doesn't let go of my hand. I've never seen so much elation concentrated in one place, lots of hugging and smiling, no one knows anyone but everyone's buzzing together.

"Come and live with me," Loïc suddenly says.

I make him repeat it, not sure if I heard right, with all this noise.

"Come and live with me. We'll do our studies together. It'll be too hard, just seeing each other at the weekend."

The crowd surges and I let go of his hand, taking advantage of the temporary distance to gather my thoughts and the pieces my heart has strewn around. I'm dying to move in with him. If I was alone, I'd leave Angoulême and my mother, and come to do my literature degree in Bordeaux. I passed my baccalauréat with distinction, my dream of becoming a schoolteacher has never been closer. I'd move into the apartment Loïc's parents are renting for his studies, we'd have student parties and evenings under the duvet, watching Buffy or Ally McBeal and eating pasta. Margaux has chosen the same course as me, we could study together. We'd spend our days in the library and on the lecture-hall benches, make new

friends, go back to Angoulême at the weekend to see our families,
and then on Sunday evening, fly back to our freedom.

The crowd has become packed. Crushing and remote at the same
time.

"And one, and two, and three, nil! And one, and two, and
three, nil!"

My life is a nil-nil match. I lean towards Loïc's ear:

"You know I can't."

"Why? Because of your sister again?"

I nod my head. He shakes his:

"She's old enough, you know. She doesn't need you to protect
her anymore."

He doesn't wait for the reply, just claps his hands and starts
chanting with the others:

"And one, and two, and three, nil! And one, and two, and
three, nil!"

7:56 A.M.

It's becoming a ritual. I'm taking up with the sea again as if it were an old friend from whom I'd grown distant over some forgotten quarrel. Every morning, the ocean's vigor gives me the courage I was lacking the previous day. I come out of the water determined to do what I came here this week to do, but, irredeemably, returning to Mima's house makes my resolutions melt away.

The sea is rough today. Encouraged by the wind, it swells, surges, rears up, curls over, then crashes down in an explosion of foam. I'm thrown around, hurled under water several times, and can barely catch my breath before a new wave plunges me back in.

When I get out, the old man is walking in my direction. I lie on my towel, exhausted. As he passes, he honors me with a friendly greeting:

"Asshole."

I sit up and give him my sweetest smile:

"Good morning, monsieur. Glad to see our relationship is blossoming."

11:43 A.M.

When I got back, Agathe was not only awake, but also dressed and overexcited.

"I've had a brilliant idea!" she declared, with all due modesty.

"Oh."

(My sister's brilliant ideas rarely live up to their billing.)

"We're going surfing! Lucas is waiting for us with some boards, on the Côte des Basques."

I tried to argue against it, explaining that the sea was raging, that they've forecast thunderstorms (not true, but must one always burden oneself with the truth?), that I hadn't had enough sleep, but Agathe had an answer to everything, and, above all, an infectious enthusiasm.

So here I am, after a scooter journey that reduced my life expectancy (Agathe clearly sees road signs as urban decoration), riding a surfboard that is itself riding a sea that's still as angry as it was this morning.

I must have been twenty the last time I surfed. I remember one boy, around my sister's age, who was also there every summer, and who really annoyed me with his tendency to finish the teacher's sentences and to succeed totally at everything I messed up. He became the famous Lucas, who's just lent us boards and wetsuits, and who now owns his own surfing school.

"Let's catch the next one!" Agathe calls out, indicating the wave that's coming.

I lie on the board and launch myself forward. I try to remain standing, but my sense of balance begs to differ. I've barely advanced a meter before I'm flattened like a pancake, cheek slapped by the wave, sinuses cleared by a squirt of seawater.

Alex is going to laugh when I tell him about this.

It's the first time in ages that I'm looking forward to talking to him. I've had it since yesterday, this feeling I no longer had. I miss him. Not just for what he provides me with and brings me, not just for all he means to me. Right now, I sense it's actually *him* I'm missing. Over time, we formed an entity: Emma-and-Alex, Alex-and-Emma, Daddy-and-Mommy, Alice-and-Sacha's parents. As the years passed, he became a part of me. I can't imagine my life without him, like I can't imagine it without my right hand. My heart tightens in my chest. I realize that I've never turned the question around. What about him, then? What does he feel?

Can he function without me? Under this surf suit, I understand, viscerally, what I'm doing here.

I took hold of Alex's hand at the very moment I let go of my little sister's hand. I left him no other choice than to help me move forward. I imposed that dependency because I needed it. If this week was necessary for me to see Agathe again, it was just as necessary for me to learn to loosen my grip on Alex.

I know he gets it. It's not like him not to call me. His style is messaging me because he's just heard our music on the radio, or phoning me to tell me the restaurant he ate in was divine. Every evening he tells me about his day and asks how mine was. Silence, for him, takes effort.

"What are you thinking about?" Agathe interrupts me, between waves.

"Nothing."

"One can't think about nothing. Well, except for our uncle. He's lacking the essential equipment."

"Absolutely. His brain has been reported missing."

"A grain of sand fell into his ear in 1990, and it's still falling."

"Worse than a black hole: the skull of Uncle Jean-Yves."

"Never seen in the same room as the Bermuda Triangle."

My stomach aches, I laugh so much. We let several waves go by before deciding to surf one. The movements come back naturally, I crouch, stand up, find my balance, and let myself be carried by the current. It's not long, three seconds at most, before I find myself head under water again, but the feeling of freedom I have during those seconds is hard to equal.

I'm pooped. We got to bed mega late because of shooting-star night—there were so many, it was like a firework display (Uncle Jean-Yves says "firework pissplay," which makes us and Jérôme laugh, but auntie not at all (don't think I've ever seen her laugh) (she must have urinary leaks, like the lady in the ad). I fell asleep in the car on the way back, Papi carried me to my bed. I thought this would mean they'd let me sleep in, but no such luck, Mima got us out of bed at the crack of dawn (10 o'clock) so we could go to our surf lesson.

The guy from the North is there, he's changed since last year. He's got long hair and pimples on his forehead (he can't know about Eau Précieuse) (I do, and it stinks). He tells me he's called Lucas, as if I'd forgotten. I've not forgotten, either, that he'd promised to write to me after snogging me behind the cabin last summer. To pay him back, I don't say a word to him all morning, and hang out with Joachim, the son of Madame Garcia (Mima's neighbor). He's nice but a bit clingy (like his hair) (never seen such greasy hair) (I think you could cook fries in it). I play it cool, but I spent hours by the phone, waiting for a call from that other moron. My mother kept telling me I was being ridiculous, I didn't go out for several weeks in case he called. Don't know how I thought he could be interested in me, I look like a doodle. My hair's curly as a sheep's, I've got fried eggs instead of boobs, toothpicks instead of legs, and a tummy that makes waves—even Picasso wouldn't have dared come up with me. It's simple: I've yet to see a girl who's uglier than me, hard as I look, but my mirror can't be argued with. And yet I found some photos of my parents when they were young, and they were great-looking (apart from their hairstyles, help!), and my sister's gorgeous.

I say I don't care, but the truth is, I'd like to be beautiful. It seems easier, everyone wants to be friends with the beautiful girls, everyone listens to what they say as if it was smarter, when it's just better packaged.

At the end of the surfing class, Joachim suggests to me that we go find some shells. At low tide there are tons, and he knows I collect them. I've got a box full of shells in my room at Mima's (Daddy's old room), and I paint gouaches of them, which are pretty. I say yes.

While I'm taking off my wetsuit, Lucas comes over to talk to me. He seems awkward, looks down at the sand, which suits me fine, that way he doesn't see the scars on my thighs. He says he wanted to phone me but my number got deleted before he had time to write it down (I'd written it on his hand). He says he's sorry, that he looked in the directory, called the info number, and found nothing, that he thought of me all year. I feel like crying and laughing all at once. He asks if I'd like to go and have an ice cream at the casino, I look over at Joachim, waiting for me on the shore, and say okay.

There's this guy who comes in every lunchtime. He takes a chicken salad sandwich and an Orangina, then goes and sits on the green seat outside Sephora to eat it. I think he works at the clothes store at the far end of the mall. He's got something of Matt Damon about him, especially when he smiles, I feel like I'm in Good Will Hunting.

There's the woman from the jewelry store, for her it's a ham sandwich, and on Wednesdays she adds a chocolate éclair. She always seems in a hurry, even on her break.

There's my favorite person, an elderly man who pops in once a week. He just comes for a tarte au sucre, and some of my news. Each time he tells me he used to work here, was even here when the Carrefour first opened.

My boss is forever breathing down my neck, but thankfully, there are the customers. To be honest, I never imagined myself working in a sandwich bar in the middle of a mall. I dreamt instead of being at university, but I'm not complaining; for the first two months, I handed out leaflets at a traffic light, and what with the people who wouldn't open their car window, and the sicko who'd drive past three times an hour with his prick on display in his Twingo, I much prefer my new job.

I rather like the Matt Damon lookalike. I wait for him to come, prepare what I'll say to him. It's him I think of when I'm putting my make-up on in the morning. It's the first time I've fancied someone since it ended with Loïc.

This lunchtime, he said something other than his order: he asked me my name. He was seriously shaking and went for it while

I was giving him change on his twenty-franc note. I left work this evening with a cash drawer that I couldn't balance and a date for the weekend.

I was smiling inanely for the entire journey home, the people on the bus must have thought me weird.

My smile disappears on the second floor. I've still got two to go and I can already hear the cries.

Agathe is in the kitchen, crouching, cowering. She's shielding her head with her arms. Mom is facing her, with her back to me. She doesn't see me arrive. "Girl, if you think you're going to speak to me like that," she says to Agathe, "you've got another think coming, no kid makes the rules under this roof." My sister moans: "I'm so sorry, Mom," but it's not enough. Mom raises her arm, her belt is wound around her hand, she's about to whip it down. It's been happening more often, with ever more force. She always apologizes afterwards, explains that it's hard bringing us up on her own, that we're not easy, that we could do our bit, and then she hugs us, calls us her darling girls, repeats that we're everything to her, that without us she'd have no reason to live anymore. Never did the thought, or even the desire, come to us to defend ourselves, to push her away. We take what's coming.

But not this time.

Anger propels me towards her, I grab her wrist, and block the blow.

Her eyes swivel onto me. She's crimson with rage. For several seconds she remains frozen, arm aloft. I tell myself that this is good, that my intervention allowed her to take stock of the situation, that she's going to put her belt back where it should be—through the loops on her trousers—and that the evening's going to proceed with apologies and a few smiles. The snap of leather on my cheek puts an end to my fantasies.

1:19 P.M.

Emma surfs as well as a *pétanque* ball. When we were kids, she was the best at it, which shows you can't take anything for granted. She keeps trying, whether out of pride or pig-headedness I don't know, and each time she ends up in the water in positions that defy gravity. She reminds me of those wall climbers with their sticky fists. I'm careful not to let slip that I surf regularly with Lucas—for once she has reason to admire me, and I'm not going to deprive her of it.

The tide has gone out, the beach is accessible once more. We come out of the water and lie on the sand to dry out.

"You're as good as you ever were," she says to me. "Do you surf often?"

"Never."

"Come on, it's obvious you practice regularly!"

"Careful, I read recently that jealousy causes piles."

She bursts out laughing:

"What nonsense!"

"Don't feel bad, it's totally normal to be jealous of my natural grace. You spent more time under the water than on the board, more sponge than surfer."

Lucas joins us for a cigarette break. His cheeks and nose are covered in green sunblock.

"So, the Delorme sisters, a good surfing session?"

Emma slaps her thigh:

"Oh, it was *surfing*? I thought it was diving we were doing!"

Lucas is enjoying this:

"Have to say, the conditions weren't brilliant, it was nicer last week. Wasn't it, Agathe?"

The jerk.

2:56 P.M.

We return the wetsuits and boards. Lucas suggests we come again tomorrow. My sister declines—surprise, surprise, she'll need some time to digest all the Atlantic she's swallowed.

She talks about him as we climb onto the scooter. "He's nicer than when we were kids," she says. "Cuter, too."

He's the only guy I've stayed friends with after trying to be more than just friends. There was a close miss as adolescents (two kisses without tongue and without sequel), then we were together in our early twenties. It followed the same trajectory as the others: a spectacular take-off, promises of everlasting love, then the crash, just as spectacular, just as drastic. It's quite simple: the sheerest pantyhose has a longer life expectancy than my love affairs. I love as quickly as I unlove. I lived with two of them, was engaged once, believed in it every time, was disappointed every time. With Lucas, it remained a beginning, just simmering, we stopped before we'd really started. He once confided in me that he was like me, a lover of extremes, an all-or-nothing type, scared of the half-hearted. There are some similarities that are best not shared, we remained friends, even if, occasionally, we find ourselves in the same bed or the same position.

I hope that one day I'll find someone who can hold on to my love. But the problem doesn't stem from others. It took me a bit of time, a few doctors, and, no doubt, the departure of my sister to understand that.

Like all the girls of my generation, I was lulled into believing in an eternal love that only death could end. Enduring couples are held up as ideals, break-ups considered failures. I'd like to live that. Part of me still hopes for that. But maybe I'm made for loving often, not for loving a long time. Maybe my heart prefers sprinting to long-distance.

For ages, I tried to mold myself to expectations, fit into the standard model, before I faced facts: I recognize myself more often in the exception than in the rule. When I do those magazine personality tests, there's never a type that corresponds to me. One day Mima told me it was just the norm that wasn't wide enough; it was a trickle of water after a drought when it should be as vast as the ocean. She was right. Norms are straitjackets, useful only for reassuring oneself by comparison. I'm not normal, I'm a limited edition. Got to admit, it's a much better look.

"Agathe! Be careful!" Emma screams in my ear.

She really is insufferable. It's hardly my fault if the traffic light turns red just when I'm lost in thought.

3:19 P.M.

There's something I'd like explained to me. Why do we always run into the people we don't want to see, but never into those we're dreaming of seeing? For example, now, coming back to Mima's, I'd have loved to find Brad Pitt (on horseback, bare-chested and with long hair, preferably, but I'd have been happy with him however, I'm not fussy). But no, it's Joachim Garcia waiting at the gate. I consider driving over him, I'd defend myself by saying I mistook him for a speed bump, but I doubt my sister would approve, so I just park sensibly.

"You've just run over my foot," he says when I get off.

"Oh, I didn't notice. Shouldn't leave it lying around. A bit like your dick."

"Hi Joachim," my traitor of a sister says, politely.

We go through the gate. I close it before he has time to follow us.

"Can we talk?" he asks.

"No, thanks."

"Agathe, I'd really like to talk to you."

I roll my eyes conspicuously and throw the keys to Emma:

"I won't be long."

He's wearing faded jeans, a white T-shirt, and sunglasses. I loathe people who don't take off their sunglasses when speaking to someone. I feel like I'm talking to a two-way mirror. His body language—hands in pockets, half-smile—says totally relaxed, all he's missing is some chewing gum.

"I sensed you were a bit tense yesterday. I thought all was forgotten, but clearly not, so I'd like to apologize if I hurt you."

I guffaw:

"*Hurt* me? You give yourself far too much importance. I'm awfully sorry if you found me cold, it's just that I didn't recognize you. You'd vanished from my memory."

"Agathe . . . "

"That is my name, yes. And yours is . . . ?"

"We were young, I was immature, it happens to everyone."

"Death does, too, but that doesn't make it acceptable."

He takes off his sunglasses. His expression is exaggeratedly sad, he's overacting, looks like a basset hound.

"It was better with the shades."

"I can see you better without them. You're still just as beautiful."

"If you could just avoid making me vomit."

Far from backing off, he keeps going:

"I heard that you'd taken it badly, that you'd done something silly. I didn't dare call you. Your grandmother didn't spare me, I thought she was going to sock me one. My mother told me she'd died recently. I'm really sorry."

Tears well up in my eyes, crying in front of him is out of the question. I'm about to go inside when a woman's voice calls him from the house next door.

"I'm coming, darling! I . . . I went to fetch something from the car, I'm hurrying!"

He turns to me: "That's my wife, she's pregnant. I'd rather avoid . . . Do you have children, yourself?"

"Yes, I've got seven, one for each day of the week, like underpants."

I don't wait for his reaction. I turn on my heel and go straight into Mima's. Emma's having a shower, I grab a handful of cereal and sit in the armchair, facing the fan.

Mom has pushed the furniture back and hung up some balloons. Everyone's here to celebrate my twentieth birthday. Mima and Papi came from Anglet, Margaux from Bordeaux, even Cyril was invited, and yet Mom can't stand him (she finds people who are too nice suspect). Also here are my gym buddies—I hadn't seen them since I finished school.

Mom had sent me off to buy her some cigarettes, stressing that I should take my time. It wasn't mega subtle, I suspected something was going on, but not this much. When I got back, they all cried out "Surprise!", like in the movies. Agathe and Mima brought in the cake: Black Forest gateau.

"Your grandmother wanted to make her tiramisu," my mother explains, seeing that I'm happy with their choice. "But I knew you preferred the Black Forest. I know my daughter well!"

Mima rolls her eyes, I wink at her. We both know, she and I, that I'd have preferred her tiramisu, it's my favorite dessert in the whole universe. I tried to make it myself one day. I followed the recipe she'd given me, step by step, the result wasn't bad, but it wasn't Mima's tiramisu. She has this knack of making the simplest dish delicious. I smile at Mom, nodding; the truth would spoil the party.

It's time for presents. The present, more exactly. A blue envelope with "Happy Birthday Emma!" written on it.

I open it, wondering what it might be and preparing to pretend to be pleased, even if I happen to be disappointed. All eyes are on me and seem impatient to discover my reaction. I realize that I'm thrilled before even reading the card.

"Voucher for driver's license."

No need to pretend, I've never received such a big present. It's crazy! They all chipped in to give it to me. I have put a little aside, but between the rent Mom asks from me and the food shopping, my wages go fast, and my boss still won't move me to full-time. Tomorrow I'm signing up at driving school!

Agathe leads me into her room, she has another present but doesn't want to give it to me in front of everyone.

From behind her bed, she pulls out a large painting of two people. I recognize us immediately. My little sister and me, her head on my shoulder, her eyes closed, my eyes on her. "It's my first painting," she tells me. She giggles, like whenever she's overcome with emotion: "I signed down there, who knows? Maybe it'll be worth millions one day!" I can't take my eyes off the canvas.

"It's worth more than millions to me," I reply.

There's a knock on the door. It's Mima and Papi, they have to go, they have a drive of nearly four hours ahead. Mima checks that the door's closed and hands me a little box. I know what I'm going to find in it, I've received an identical box every year since my birth. Inside, a cultured pearl.

"It's the most important one," Mima murmurs, stroking the necklace around her neck, "because it's the last one. I feel very emotional, my darling girl."

I do, too. It's a tradition Mima's continued from her own grandmother. Every year, until Mima's twentieth birthday, she gave her a pearl. The twenty pearls were then strung into a necklace.

"It never leaves me," Mima often told me.

She strokes my cheek. "My first granddaughter, my darling girl. Twenty, already. You know that, when you were born, I was forty-eight? When I'd walk you in your baby carriage, people took me for your mother, and I must admit, I didn't always correct them."

I throw myself into her arms. I love her so much. Without her, without Papi, I don't know what my life would have been like. Summers with them were always the colorful interlude to all the *grayness. I don't tell them about the daily hell, so as not to worry them, to protect Mom, but I know that they know, that they sense it. That they see the marks. Several times, Mima asked me questions. I lied. She respected that, but with a seriousness I'd never heard from her, she told me: "Just one word, one sign, and you both come and live here."*

Papi died yesterday. Mom decided I should come home, to leave Mima in peace, but me abandoning her was out of the question. Emma is on vacation with Cyril, she's making her way here to join us.

My heart's in pieces. I can't believe I'll never see him again. Even worse, I can't believe Mima will never see him again. He set off yesterday morning, and then, just like that, a heart attack, all over. It's Mima I've been thinking of since I heard. I didn't even faint, which I usually do at any intense emotion, and as far as intense emotions go, this one's right up there.

The doctor gave her something to help her sleep. I spent the night beside her. She said Papi's name several times during the night, and Daddy's name, too. I realized that I'd never really considered what she had felt when he died.

She's still asleep when I get up, which never happens. I prepare breakfast for her, the same breakfast she makes us every morning: slices of toast with salted butter. I make her a coffee—coffee is so rank, but so are cigarettes, and I still smoke them, pinching Peter Stuyvesants from Mom's bag.)

The bedroom is dark, I leave the door open to let light in from the corridor. The floorboards creak, Mima opens her eyes. She's still dressed, her outfit from yesterday. I place the tray at the foot of the bed and slide up beside her. She smiles at me, strokes my cheek, and then, suddenly, I can see the devastation in her eyes. For a few seconds she'd forgotten, and reality has just caught up with her.

I snuggle up to her, like when I was little and she'd console me whenever I was sad. She weeps, her body shakes. I don't know *what to do to comfort her, I stroke her hair, wipe her cheeks, it's the first time I've had to console someone other than myself, and it has to be Mima. I didn't know one could feel the suffering of someone else so intensely. I don't know what to do with all this pain, I'd like to throw it out, turn back the clock, bring back Papi and Mima's smile. I'd do anything for her to feel better, not only for her, but also for me, because I can't imagine her not being okay, her disappearing, too. I couldn't bear having to do without her one day.*

I get up and hand her the coffee. She calms down a little, breathes in the aroma, closes her eyes. I pinch a slice of her toast. She hugs me.

"Thank you, my little darling."

"I didn't put in any sugar, want some?"

"It's not for the coffee that I'm thanking you. It's for your love. You've already worked it all out, you know that love is the only remedy for grief. It's all that counts, in the end: making yourself a place in the hearts of others, and welcoming others into your own. You're special, my darling. You put your emotions before your reason, don't ever lose that."

I'm trying not to cry, but she's not helping me.

"Thank you, Mima. But all the same, I'm not sure I want to be special. Mom says life's easier when you have no heart, maybe she's right. At least if you love no one, you lose no one and you're never sad."

She smiles, I thought that would never happen again.

"My darling, I'd rather suffer until the end of my days because I've lost your grandfather than never have known him."

"But if you'd never known him, you wouldn't be sad."

"I'd be sad not to have known him."

"You'd feel nothing since you wouldn't know him."

"You'll understand when you're older."

I hate that sentence adults resort to when they've run out of arguments. I hope Mima's right, that it's a good thing to be like I am, because sometimes I feel like my heart's taking up all the space in my body, and that doesn't make breathing easy.

5:06 P.M.

An entire wall of my father's old room is covered in videos. Papi was a movie buff. At the beginning of each week, when he received the TV listings he and Mima subscribed to, he'd mark up the movies that interested him. He'd program his VCR to record them, then cut out the insert with the summary, review, and still, and slip this information into the cassette cover. On the spine he'd write the title and a number. The procedure was then almost complete. He'd just have to open his black book at the page of the first letter in the title and add the movie and its number after those that preceded it. The book—and the shelves—contained several hundred movies, most missing a bit of the beginning or the end, despite the margin of error Papi allowed for when programing the recording. I can still see him moaning about those confounded ads delaying everything.

Right at the bottom of the shelves, some smaller cassettes are classified by year. I grab the one for 1996.

"D'you know what this is?" I ask Agathe.

"Papi's own videos. Don't you remember him filming everything with his camcorder?"

The memory comes back to me, as if aroused from a long sleep. Our grandfather's craggy face, his laughing eye behind his black camcorder.

"D'you think we could watch them?"

"I know Mima sometimes did," my sister replies. "She'd insert the small cassette into a bigger one. Hey, look, there it is!"

She pulls a VHS cassette from the shelf. A rectangular slot at its center holds the 1996 cassette perfectly.

"D'you think the video player still works?"

"Let's give it a go!"

6:01 P.M.

It took us nearly an hour. The video player had clearly not been used for some time, the remote control had gone missing, and the TV didn't recognize the contraption. But we're off. The image is dated, the composition random, the interest of the subject relative: the past appears on the screen.

Rome's Coliseum and Papi's voice in the background.

"January 14 1996. We arrived in Rome this morning after a long bus journey. The first organized visit is the Coliseum, and I must say, I didn't imagine it being this impressive. Just look at the architecture . . . oh, hold on, why's the camcorder making that noise? No way! It can't let me down on the first day! And I paid a small fortune for it, too. Darling, can you believe it? The salesman told me it was indestructible, and it's already playing up."

Mima's voice.

"Darling, I'm going to tell you just the once: I don't want to hear you moaning about your equipment. You know what I think about it, it's forever breaking down, it annoys you, and it spoils your enjoyment. Just make the most of this using your eyes."

"I knew I could count on you."

"At your service, darling."

We crack up laughing. I'd forgotten how much those two loved joshing each other.

"Rewind, I want to hear Mima again!" Agathe says.

We listen to it three times, before continuing with the Rome visit. Then the screen goes dark and we're in March. Mima's sitting at the table in the sitting room, Uncle Jean-Yves comes out of the kitchen holding a cake with lit candles. Everyone starts singing "Happy Birthday," with Papi's voice drowning out the rest—that was his thing, booming like a tenor to amuse everyone.

Agathe sits deeper in the armchair and draws up her legs.

Once again, the dark screen, we're now in July. From the garden, a static shot of the glass doors to the sitting room. Papi sighs: "D'you think they're going to be long? I'm using up film waiting for them." Mima replies: "I'd remind you that you filmed the mayor's speech after his election—even a roughcast wall's more interesting. Ah, here they are!"

Here we are indeed. I'm wearing jeans ripped at the knees and a pink top showing my belly button, and Agathe's in a yellow flounced skirt and crochet top. "Go on, put the music on," the eleven-year-old Agathe tells me. The sixteen-year-old me presses the switch on the player, Ophélie Winter starts to sing, and we start to dance.

"*J'étais assise sur une pierre / Des larmes coulaient sur mon visage / Je ne savais plus comment faire / Où trouver en moi le courage . . .*"

I'm torn between wanting to disappear into the ground and wanting to go and hug those two girls, who are still innocent enough to put their own pleasure before the opinions of others.

"My god, did we really do that?" Agathe guffaws, looking at the screen between her fingers.

"We were the queens of choreography, we'd do it at the drop of a hat, don't you remember?"

"Of course I do, to my regret. It's better to forget some things. Like that crocheted top, seriously, it looks like a doily. Who'd wear that, apart from a pedestal table?"

"Just look at your little face, with your blond curls. You were too cute! Sometimes, I'd rather like to go back to those days."

Agathe stretches out her legs and puts her feet on the coffee table:

"I wouldn't."

I suddenly realize that it was at that age that she started being in a really bad way. Not long after, she stopped wearing skirts. I discovered one day, going into her room without knocking, that she was hiding the signs of cutting on her thighs.

I change the subject:

"D'you know, I recently discovered that I'd been getting Ophélie Winter's lyrics wrong? For years I sang *'Dieu m'a donné la foi, un qui je ne sais quoi.'* She actually says *'un p'tit je ne sais quoi.'* When I think of all the parties at which I sang that, at the top of my voice, I dread to think of all the people I made a fool of myself in front of."

As I expected, my sister doesn't hold back from laughing.

"I know! Personally, it was an Axelle Red song that I slaughtered for years. She says: *'Laisse-moi être fan,'* and until very recently I'd sing: *'Laisse ma raie, Stéphane.'*"

I almost choke:

"But surely you must have suspected she wasn't really saying that?"

"Well, I don't see why not! I've sometimes said that kind of thing."

My stomach aches, I'm laughing so hard. Agathe's in tears. When we finally regain our composure, several minutes later, we put on the 1990 cassette. We don't pick it at random, we know what we're going to find on it. We know *who* we're going to find on it.

He appears within the first few seconds, in swimming trunks on the beach. He's playing racquetball with his brother, Uncle Jean-Yves. The ball always lands too far away, Dad pretends to grumble. "Don't know why I keep playing with him, he's got two left hands," he says to Papi, who's filming.

"I'd forgotten his voice," Agathe murmurs.

I had, too. I'd hear one, in my memories, but it wasn't like the one in the video.

I'm happy to hear him, see him. For a moment, I feel as if he's not far away. Then Dad's death comes back to me. I know the void it left me with. It's tricky, growing up straight when the foundations are missing.

Then I think about my own children. I miss them. It's abrupt, immediate, my need for them is physical. It starts in the belly and floods over me, everything becomes confused, suddenly the emotions taking me over can't be untangled.

Since being a mother, I view my childhood differently. More gently, more compassionately. More admiringly, too. I never complained, was never disturbed by all I'd been through, never thought my life was harder than any other life. It's when I imagine my children in my position that I feel the fear, the sadness, the injustice of certain scenarios. By showering them with love, part of me is consoling the child I was.

"How about we go to a club this evening?" Agathe suddenly asks.

She wrenches me from my thoughts. My heart returns to its normal rhythm.

"To a club? A nightclub?"

"No, a golf club. Of course, a nightclub! It's years since I last went to one. D'you fancy it?"

I don't fancy it one bit. I never liked clubbing, even at the age I was supposed to like it. I'd go with my friends and invariably end up falling asleep on a banquette, despite the music and cigarette smoke. I'm about to say no, but then, like whenever I've been ready to say no this week, I think of the reasons that pushed me to suggest this vacation to Agathe, and I say yes.

I couldn't get out of bed this morning. It's the third time since term started. I set two alarm clocks, one at the other end of my room, but then switch them off before going back to sleep. I can sleep until midday, even longer if I try. Sleep is my oblivion.

Thank goodness my Mom leaves early, or it would be war. I fake her signature in my grade book, but I can tell the principal is starting to ask questions. He mustn't call her in because, try as I might, I can't fake her physical appearance.

I don't understand why I'm like this. Fatigue deadens my brain and body, I'm incapable of moving and thinking, all I want is to sleep. Whatever the consequences. I got a two-hour detention because I dozed off in geography. I'd asked Sonia to wake me up if the teacher realized I was sleeping, but seeing as I was snoring and it was making everyone laugh, she let me get caught (next time she's got something stuck in her teeth, I won't let her know).

It's after two o'clock when I surface. I get dressed, pour myself a bowl of Cocoa Krispies, tidy everything away to leave no trace, and sit in front of the TV. I zap but there's nothing on except stuff for old people, and I end up with a serial on TF1. I often watch dumb programs, but I still want to know the ending, so I'm obliged to keep watching until then. But this time, I'll never know the ending. Just when I was about to find out if Brenda would finally have it off with Jason, a special announcement cuts into the program and a journalist announces that an accident has taken place in the United States. The images are terrible. A tower is in flames, a mass of black smoke escaping from it. Suddenly, a plane plunges into the second tower, which also explodes. I can't believe it, I'm stunned.

I watch the images again and again, I can't tear my eyes from the screen. I can't stand up, I'm struggling to breathe. My whole body is shaking. They announce that there's been another plane, it's crashed into the Pentagon. Then a fourth, into a field. They talk of an attack. I don't know how long I remain there, shocked, my bowl of soggy cereal untouched on the coffee table. The two towers collapsed.

Emma comes home from work, she already knows. She ran here as soon as the sandwich bar closed. "I wanted to be with you," she tells me. Mom gets in later, she's crying, she takes us in her arms. She doesn't notice that my shoes and backpack haven't budged since yesterday.

Night falls. We eat cereal in front of the TV. There's new footage, people smothered in ash, screams, deaths. I'm not ready for it. I'm not ready to watch that world. I want to go back to childhood, even if mine wasn't perfect, when my main concern was Barbie's outfit, when adults would speak in hushed voices so I wouldn't hear about dramas, when I believed that the dead lived up in the sky, when the world was just my family. I don't feel up to it. Living sometimes seems like an insurmountable effort. I return to sleeping.

C yril dumped me. I was just playing Snake on my Nokia when I got an SMS.
"Itz over."
I had no credit left to call him and Mom didn't want me calling him from the landline, so I went over to his place to talk. He was with his friend Kader, but he let me come in. He was distant, like he was a stranger, while I was trying my best not to cry, without success.

I asked why, what I'd done wrong, he said he'd had enough, that he wanted to move on to something else. I'm sure he's got someone else, it makes no sense otherwise. Recently, we celebrated a year together. He said he wanted to live with me and, again last week, he was saying he'd love me for life. I was one of his three favorite phone numbers for his "millennium tariff," which is a commitment, of sorts.

I tried to make him change his mind, but he clearly felt like playing Sims with Kader more than giving me some explanation. He didn't even notice that I'd left.

I walk home, I'm crying too much to take the bus and risk bumping into someone. It's raining, I've got frozen fingers and a stomachache. I've rarely wanted to be home this badly.

I don't know if I'll be able to get over it. I've never loved anyone like I love him. I even practiced signing with his surname. We work in the same place, me at the sandwich bar, him at the clothes store, I'll run into him every day, which won't help with healing.

Mom's at work. I charge straight into Agathe's room. She's busy bleaching her moustache while listening to Britney Spears. She immediately notices the state I'm in, puts down her cotton pad and takes me into her arms.

"What's going on?"

"Cyril's ditched me."

"D'you want me to go and smash his face in?"

I say no. She's capable of it. I cry liters of tears, feels like they're never going to stop, as if a cloud has followed me inside and decided never to leave me.

Agathe checks her radio-alarm and pulls on her bomber jacket.

"You're going?"

"Yes, Sonia's waiting for me at the newsstand. We're going to Benoît's, the whole gang's there. Want to come?"

"Can't face seeing people. You don't fancy taking in a movie, the two of us? I'd like to see Bridget Jones's Diary, it's supposed to be great."

She ties her hair into a tight ponytail, then pulls out two fine strands to frame her face.

"I'm really sorry, Emma, I'd really like to."

I don't believe this. She can't have understood how bad I'm feeling, she can't leave me alone when my heart's in a thousand pieces, just to go and see the friends she sees every day.

Never could I do that to her.

"Gagathe, please. Could you stay with me?"

She stops, considers, and sits down beside me on her bed:

"Sonia's waiting for me, things aren't going great with her guy. She needs me. I'll be back early, promise."

11:30 P.M.

I've rarely felt so old. Since the club I used to frequent no longer exists, we searched on the Net for somewhere to go dancing. We chose the highest rated one, a club right in the center of Biarritz. We got ready (in my case, I went to town on the make-up, and I've got so much highlighter on my cheekbones, an astronaut could spot me from outer space,) and we turned up there in all innocence, not suspecting how ancient it was going to make us feel.

"I haven't been to a discotheque for twenty years," Emma says, going through the door.

The bouncers are amused.

"Emma, no one says discotheque anymore, not since the last century."

"Oh? Can one still say 'dance hall'?"

I must pull quite a face because she feels obliged to clarify that she's joking.

The dance floor is empty when we arrive. We go up to the bar, a barman comes to take our order.

"There's no one here?" Emma asks him.

"You're the first!" he replies. "It's really early, people arrive later."

A detail I'd left in the past. And anyhow, if I'd listened to Emma, we'd have turned up at ten. The barman puts our drinks on the bar and goes off again, to set up.

"I bet you like him," Emma whispers to me, with a wink.

"Come off it, he's twelve years old, I bet he has a ruler in his pocket. You could be his grandmother."

She doesn't hit back. It's not like her to ignore an open goal. Since late afternoon, I've sensed that she was elsewhere, absent.

"D'you want to go?" I ask.

She hesitates for a few seconds, seems to be debating with herself, then heads for the dance floor:

"No way. My decrepit body needs to dance!"

I follow her. I don't know the track that's playing, some kind of electronic music with a fast beat, a groove I definitely can't dance to. I'm used to rock, R&B, pop, I move my head and arms, trying to follow the rhythm. Emma seems even more lost than me. She waddles timidly, looks like she needs to pee. I regret having the idea, don't know what the hell we're doing here. We won't stay long, one or two tracks and we'll be off.

12:53 A.M.

Emma's in a trance. If I hadn't been right beside her all night, I'd swear she'd taken something (and I don't mean a chamomile tea). In the middle of the floor, now packed, she's been dancing non-stop for over an hour. Her moves are expansive, surprisingly fluid, as if she's back in control of her body. As for me, my heart imposes regular breaks, and makes it clear that, if I demand too much of it, it could exercise its right to go on strike.

A guy accosts me as I'm downing a drink, perched on an armchair:

"Hi. May I sit with you?"

I note the refinement of the approach but can't decently allow myself to be accosted by a kid.

"That's nice, but I'm going back to dance," I reply.

"Might we dance together?"

"What's your name?"

"Léo."

"Léo, I'm touched by your interest in me. But I only go out with men who are no longer eating baby formula."

He laughs, high-fives me, and moves off. The DJ drops a new

track, Emma's still dancing, eyes closed, transported by the music, impervious to what's going on around her. When a ray of light hits her face, I glimpse a smile. I put my glass down and go and join her.

"All good?" I ask in her ear.

She opens her eyes wide, surprised to find me there.

"Oh, Agathe, you had a wonderful idea, it's doing me so much good!"

"You need to do yourself good at the moment?"

She stops for a moment, looks me gently in the eye, takes my hand:

"Dance with me, Gagathe. Tonight, we forget everything."

There's something about her voice, her tone, that leaves me no choice. So, I dance. I don't close my eyes, I keep them on her, and I choke with emotion. It's as if, in the deafening music, under the blinding lights, after three days of sniffing and turning around each other, I'm really seeing her. By letting go, Emma is here. Five years have passed. On this night, I get my big sister back.

The homeroom teacher calls me up at the end of class. I'm expecting her to blast me for my absence last week, but no, she wants to congratulate me. "For the past two weeks, all your teachers have noticed a change in your behavior. You're participating, you show that you're willing, and your grades reflect that. Monsieur Loste told me you got 18/20 in math, that will raise your average."

I get home first. Emma's still at work, and Mom's still in rehab. She says that, this time, it's going to work. Personally, I've decided to stop hoping. At the end of hope there's only disappointment. Although, deep inside, I still believe in it a little. She's home tomorrow, I can't wait, even if it is calmer when she's not here. I tidy up the apartment, vacuum clean, and while I'm at it, do the windows. She'll be pleased.

I've been in great form for a while now. I think that's finally it, adolescence over and done with! Or it's because I'm going out with Kamel. I've never been in love this way, it's crazee, I want to be with him all the time. He lives far away, I have to take three buses to see him, but it's worth it. He gave me the CD of Moulin Rouge, I listen to it non-stop and think of him. I'm sure he's the man of my life.

Every Saturday, I go and support him at his rugby matches, and after, there are post-match celebrations with the team and their girlfriends. Everyone loves me, I organize games and activities, which they all enjoy. We often end up at a nightclub, and I dance for hours, without stopping, until closing time, and if I could, I'd keep going. I'm always the last out, the bouncers call me by my first name.

While waiting for Emma, I put pop videos on TV, grab a pack of cookies, some Gruyère, chips, and a glass of cola, and settle in the sitting room to get on with my project. I've been working on it for three weeks now, every day and into the night. Until I'm fit to drop, in other words. I draw silhouettes, dresses, trousers, corsets, pumps, boots. It was seeing Jean Paul Gaultier on TV that gave me the idea. He seems such a nice guy! Once I've finished, I'll send him my drawings, I'm sure he'll call me so we can work together. I don't know how I never thought of it before—it's obvious that I'm cut out for it.

Emma gets in at six. There are loose sheets of paper all over the sitting room. She rolls her eyes and heads straight for the shower. I know what she thinks, but she's wrong. She says Jean Paul Gaultier doesn't give a fig about my drawings, he won't even get to see them. She says it's for my own good, that one mustn't have dreams that are too big, or they take up more room than real life. She says she doesn't want me to be disappointed. She's jealous. I won't be disappointed, I'm sure I'm right. Jean Paul Gaultier will love my drawings, he'll beg me to work with him, I'll go off to live in Paris with Kamel, and my mother, Mima, and Emma will be proud of me.

I quit my job. My boss was forcing me to take my vacation in September, which would have meant canceling summer at Mima's. Last year, I only got two weeks, which was tough but better than nothing. All year, I count the days separating me from my grandmother, so waiting until September to go there was unthinkable.

My mother was really pissed, threatening to throw me out if I can't pay my share of the rent. I promised her I'd find another job in September, but the truth is, I'm dreaming of just one thing: leaving. I can't stand her fits of anger. She hasn't raised a hand to me for a while now, apparently moving into the adults' camp has given me a kind of immunity, but she doesn't hold back with Agathe. All my life, I've been scared of her, found excuses for her, but now I can feel anger taking over. I don't know how long I can hold out. It's intolerable being dependent on her moods, dreading her return every evening, being careful about everything one says, how one says it, how one looks at her, how one walks.

"Would you like some dessert?" Mima asks me.

The whole family is around the table under the linden tree to celebrate Uncle Jean-Yves's birthday. Mima hands me a serving of tiramisu, she knows I can't resist it.

"Agathe should have some, too," Aunt Geneviève comments.

"I already said I didn't want any," my sister retorts.

"You don't need to take that tone, it was to do you a favor. You're thin as a toothpick and you eat nothing."

Agathe rolls her eyes. I rest my hand on her arm so she knows I'm with her, even though I'm starting to lose my patience with her character. The start of the vacation was perfect, but for a few days now, she's been odious with everyone.

"Come on, darling," Mima steps in. "A small serving and you won't be nagged anymore."

Agathe suddenly stands up:

"Get off my fucking back, all of you!"

"Want to repeat that?" my uncle roars, standing up himself.

"D'you really think you scare me?" Agathe sniggers. "I said: 'Get off my fucking back!' I'm not bugging anyone, I'm in my corner, and you all keep attacking me the whole time. I've had it up to here with you! Leave me alone, for fuck's sake!"

She runs off and slams the gate. Silence descends around the table. For several seconds, everyone seems stunned.

"I always thought that girl would turn out difficult," Uncle Jean-Yves finally says, sitting back down.

"She doesn't have an easy life," Mima reasons.

"Mom, stop finding excuses for her! It's not helping her. In our family, we don't behave like that, and there's no reason to start now."

"She reminds me of her mother," Geneviève says. She glances at me, then adds:

"Fortunately, you're not like the two of them."

I lower my head, I'm ashamed. Ashamed of not defending my sister, not explaining to them that she's great, deep down. That I know no one more generous, sensitive, and empathetic than her. That occasionally, things do boil over, and she doesn't know how to cope. Ashamed of not screaming at them that she's nothing like our mother, that she's never hurt anyone, that the only person she harms is herself. Ashamed, more than anything, because, deep inside me, I'm starting to think like them.

3:14 A.M.

I let the scalding water run down my nape. I'm freezing cold, can't seem to warm up. And yet, in the middle of the night, Mima's thermometer still reads 28°C.

Agathe did fall asleep. I didn't think she'd manage to. Getting into a serious discussion at two in the morning wasn't exactly a brilliant idea.

She was already annoyed when we left the club. In the cloak-room, she bumped into a friend who, introductions barely over, was determined to inform her that her ex, Mathieu, was coupled up. On the way home, she kept on about it. "The bastard, he didn't hang around. I'm sure he was already with her, that's why he dumped me, but he's such a coward, he preferred to put the blame on me. I hope she gives him more fungal infections than there are mushrooms on a Regina pizza." While driving, I tried to defuse things:

"Maybe your friend got it wrong."

"No way, he told me the girl's name, and I'm not even sur-prised. Don't know any girl as hot for it as her. She defrosts her windshield by sitting on it."

"Calm down, Agathe, you're just hurting yourself."

"I'm just telling the truth. I don't judge, you can do whatever you like, but it's a fact: that girl has seen more sausages than a barbecue."

"Then he wasn't the right guy. You know what they say? Plenty more fish in the sea."

The moment the words left my lips, I wondered why I'd said

them. I know few expressions as dumb as that one. But I never imagined they could make Agathe that furious. Her volume went up a notch, she was almost shouting:

"Seriously, Emma? That's all you could come up with? You really think people are interchangeable? You really think other 'fish' will make me forget the man I love? I don't even know why it surprises me, it totally follows that you'd think that."

I didn't respond, I knew exactly what she was implying. She went silent for a moment, maybe trying to keep in what she was dying to say, then she came out with it:

"Is that what you told yourself, when you threw me out of your life? That I could just replace you?"

She burst into tears and slammed the dashboard.

"Stop the car, I want to get out."

I made as if I hadn't heard her. No way was I leaving her on the edge of the road in the middle of the night. She started to scream:

"EMMA! LET ME OUT FOR FUCK'S SAKE!"

"Calm down, Gagathe."

"DON'T CALL ME THAT! YOU ABANDONED ME, DON'T PRETEND WE'RE STILL CLOSE!"

I said nothing more. Her fits of rage have always paralyzed me, I know it's best to just wait for them to pass.

I'd hardly come to a stop outside Mima's when she shot out of the car. She went into the house, slammed the door, and flew up to her room. From the garden, I could hear her sobbing.

I waited for silence to return, and then joined her. She was curled up in a ball on her bed, her face covered in mascara.

"I'm so sorry," she said.

"It's not your fault, Gagathe."

"You know about it?"

I nodded my head:

"Mima told me."

She sits up:

"I got the diagnosis three years ago. It wasn't exactly the surprise of the century; I knew what they were going to tell me. Bipolar 2."

"It must have been a shock."

"A bit, of course. I'd have preferred not to have to take medication for life, and when I say I'm bipolar, people are scared. But more than anything, it was a feeling of enormous relief. For a start, it explained those periods when I barely had the strength to get out of bed, and those when I was hyper, and my fits of anger, too; in short, it relieved me of oppressive guilt. But mainly, it meant there was a treatment and, if it worked, maybe I'd have a more normal life. It took time to find the ideal dosage, at first it got worse, and there are quite a few side effects and still a few ups and downs, but I'm alive again."

She paused, looked at me intently. She was waiting for my reaction. When Mima told me about my sister's disorder, I wasn't surprised, either. I always knew. It wasn't conscious, more like a visceral or animal instinct, but from birth, I sensed a flaw, a fragility in Agathe. She walked on the edge of the abyss. She was ruled by her emotions, at the mercy of her moods. That's doubtless why, naturally, I tried to shield her. I feared that the slightest knock would break her. Giving a name to Agathe's disorder allows me to understand her better, but in my eyes, the diagnosis changes nothing. Bipolarity doesn't define her, it's a part of her.

I rested my head on her shoulder:

"I'm happy that you're reassured. I can see it, I can sense it. But admit it, you've mainly found a good excuse to be able to shout at me."

I'm eighteen today. Romain is there waiting for me, after school. I can hear him from a distance, he's listening to 50 Cent at full blast in his Clio. I daren't tell him that it's not my thing, I prefer Kyo (I've been listening to "Dernière danse" non-stop since it was released.) I don't want to disappoint him, he's the man of my life. I've never felt this way. Emma claims I said the same thing about Kamel and Manu; maybe, but it was nothing like this. Romain's just perfect.

I can't believe he was interested in me. He's gorgeous, trustworthy, he could go out with stunners. I don't know what he sees in me. I've got a nose so long it's a wonder I don't tilt forward, and Nellie Olesen's hair and crooked teeth. On top of that, I've piled two kilos back on since last summer, I'm massive, I have to wear an L. Mom keeps a close eye on me while I'm eating, she caught me emptying my plate out of the window. She told the doctor about it, don't know what he said to her, but now she won't leave me alone. It's pretty crazy, not being able to do what I want with my own body!

I didn't know Romain was coming to pick me up, he did it to surprise me. He tells me to jump in, that we're going to his place. I go, but I must watch the time, Mom's planned a cake, and before that we'll go to the restaurant, like every year, and if I'm home late, she'll go crazy.

He gives me a two-track CD of Avril Lavigne. "I'd like it if you wore crop tops like her," he says.

We have sex. It always hurts me a bit, I can't seem to relax. I'd like him to take his time, for it to be over less quickly, but I don't dare tell him.

He takes me home on time. Mom and Emma are there, they sing "Happy Birthday."

After the restaurant, Mom gets the photo albums out, and starts blubbing at pictures of me as a baby.

"I know I was ugly, but all the same, control yourself!" I say, laughing.

"It's true you were ugly," Emma confirms. "That's what I thought on seeing you for the first time."

"It went by so fast," my mother moans. "I'd like to rewind, I'd do things differently."

We spend a while looking at the photos, then the cake arrives. I get to have a sharing-sized millefeuille.

"The biggest slice for the star of the day!" Mom says as she serves me.

She doesn't take her eyes off me, I eat it all, to the very last mouthful. It's delicious. I like the top part best. I could eat the tops of millefeuilles all day long.

But if I do that, I won't be able to wear a crop top.

Mom puts the music on. Emma takes another slice of cake. I go to the bathroom, I think of my flat stomach, and shove my fingers down my throat.

We left.
It was the final straw.
Mom was uncontrollable.
I thought she was going to kill Agathe.
I threw our things into a bag.
We took the bus, then the train.

Mima opens the door to us.
Agathe starts to cry, I do, too.
"Come in, my darling girls."

9:23 A.M.

I don't feel like getting out of bed. Just three more days to go and it'll be over. Emma keeps knocking on my door and my only response is a grunt.

I don't know how I managed all this time without her.

When I was fifteen, I broke my wrist. I fell over, put my hands out to stop myself, and heard a crack. The pain was so intense I felt nothing. Apparently, that's what happens when something's too painful, the brain blocks out the information. Well, my brain blocked out how much I missed my sister. I spent five years being able to live without her because my inability to live without her was so painful.

When she suggested this week together, my initial reaction was to think "out of the question." I took five days to reply to her, to persuade myself it might be a good idea. In the days leading up to it, I spurred myself on, like before some trial one could do without. Finally, I rolled up acting happy, even though it felt false. As soon as I saw her, my armor just fell apart. And today, it has completely disappeared. My sister and Mima are the only two people I allowed myself to be myself with. No control, no artifice. Stark naked. This naturalness is coming back to me. Last night, on the dance floor, I felt that connection we'd always had. I never want to lose it ever again.

9:42 A.M.

She sticks her head round the door.

"Get up, lazy bones!"

"Hmmm."

"Come on, I've got a surprise for you!"

She comes into the room and opens the shutters. I bury my face in the pillow:

"No way am I climbing the Rhune."

She laughs.

"Promise, it'll be more fun. Come on, get out of bed, we're going to be late."

10:15 A.M.

We're driving towards Biarritz, Emma's at the wheel. Since getting up, I've been trying to find out where she's taking me.

"Is it something you can eat?"

"Not telling you."

"You can lick?"

"Agathe!"

"I was thinking of an ice cream, you shameless hussy."

"Of course."

"Is it a sport?"

"Don't know."

"Are we going to the movies?"

"You're wasting your time."

I give up, I'd have more chance getting Zorro's Bernardo to talk.

The sight of a ginormous spider making its way across the dashboard puts an abrupt stop to my questions.

What am I saying, a spider?

A monster.

A crab.

Brown with great big legs. It's heading straight for me.

I scream, Emma jumps.

"STOP DRIVING! STOP IMMEDIATELY!"

"What? But why?"

"STOPPP DRIVINGGG!"

Unaware of the danger, she takes the time to leave the traffic circle and pulls up at the edge of the road. As a level-headed and responsible person, I eject from the car like bread from a toaster, and find myself on the sidewalk, legs in vibration mode. I can't tear my eyes away from the beast, which is calmly continuing its tour of the car. My sister sees it, lets out a death-rattle cry, and catapults herself out, too.

"What do we do now?" she asks, hiding behind me.

"We set fire to the car."

Her silence makes me think she's seriously contemplating it.

"I'm not getting back in while it hasn't got out. It's the spider or me."

"Tell it that, maybe it'll hear you."

I said that for a laugh, but Emma's sense of humor has clearly remained on the driving seat. She takes one step towards the car and glares at the creature, which has stopped moving. A face-off ensues, the tension is at its height:

"It's you or me, bitch. And I'm stronger than you."

"If that doesn't scare it . . . "

The spider isn't done yet and advances towards the car door. My sister jumps backwards and, almost in tears, says:

"Please, get out! I'll do whatever you want!"

It's too much for me, I crack up laughing. She tries to keep a straight face but can't resist for long. The two of us find ourselves crying with laughter on the sidewalk, facing a spider that's eyeing us with disdain.

10:29 A.M.

Thanks to the intervention of a passer-by, who ushered the spider out of the car using a book, we were able continue on our way. We arrive just in time at the thalassotherapy center, where Emma has booked us in for a massage.

"I thought it was just what we needed," she says.

I let myself be led into a cubicle, while she goes off to another one. It's the first time in my life that I'll be having a massage. The masseuse tells me I must put on the paper briefs that are on the table and lie down, then she leaves me alone. I get undressed, hang my clothes on the rail, switch my phone to silent, and take the aforementioned briefs out of the wrapper. The problem is immediately apparent: I don't know which way round to wear this thing. I mean, I'm not far off forty, I've worn quite a few undies in my life—body-shapers, G-strings, tummy-flatteners, pure cotton ones, lacy ones, shorties, tangas, bodysuits—but something like this, never. The front and back are the same width, and the makers seemingly ran out of funds. It's a double G-string, which could suit people with a double ass, but unfortunately that's not me. I bet if I farted, it would whistle, like when you press an acacia leaf to your mouth. I wonder which part of the anatomy it's supposed to conceal. Maybe I misunderstood, maybe she didn't say "briefs," but rather, "hairband."

There's a tap on the door. Time I got ready.

I put my pubic hairband on as best I can, and the masseuse returns.

"Would you prefer a relaxing massage or an energizing one?"

"What's the difference?"

"The relaxing massage relaxes, and the energizing massage energizes."

I go for the one that energizes.

The minute she starts, I regret not having chosen the relaxing one.

The lecture hall is huge, but there are so many of us, some students are sitting on the floor. It's the second day of the course and I've already made a friend. She's called Maria and lives in the studio apartment above mine. She spoke to her boss about me, and tomorrow I've got an interview to work at McDonald's. Can't wait to tell Mima about it. I know she does it gladly, but I also know that my rent is a massive drain on her small pension.

I struggle to write everything down, the history-of-literature lecturer speaks far too fast. He warned us from the start: only write notes on what's essential, but everything seems essential to me.

"Don't bother writing notes, I've already got the lectures," my neighbor whispers to me.

He must see my questioning look, so adds, "It's my second first year." Then, "I'm Alex, and you are?"

For lunch yesterday, I had a ham sandwich on a bench; today, the peak of luxury: I'm eating in the cafeteria. Maria comes with me. She tells me her background, how she left Spain to study here; I only half-listen while gazing around me. I can't get over it. I'm here. After years of dreaming about it, I'm living it.

My phone rings. I don't answer, I know who it is. My mother has been leaving us both ten messages a day since we left. She's apologized, threatened to come and "grab us by the scruff of our asses," to commit suicide, she's cried, shouted, but neither I nor my sister has ever called her back. It's hard. I often feel like forgiving her, believing her when she swears she's understood, when she promises she's changed. When you love someone, it's easier to believe them than to believe reality. I will come round to talking to her again, but I need time.

Alex is smoking outside the cafeteria. He probably thinks he seems casual, but I saw him slowing down when he spotted me.
"Where are you from?" he asks.
"Anglet."
"Cool! I love the Basque Country."
"Cool."
"Great. Want a cig?"
"I don't smoke."
"Right. Well, then, see ya!"
"Bye!"
He moves off, Marie is amused:
"That was one scintillating conversation!"
I laugh, too, but without taking my eyes off Alex's cute little ass.

Agathe is already home when I get back, sprawled on the sofa-bed we share at night, polishing off a bag of chips while watching Friends.
"So, good second day?" she asks.
"Great! And your day?"
"Ace! I've found a job! I'll be cleaning at a tech company, four evenings a week."
Her classes at the social-work school started last month, and she seems to enjoy them. She's made a gang of friends; I've not seen her thriving like this for ages. The summer at Mima's was tricky, doubtless a reaction to us leaving Mom's. She spent lots of time in her room, listening to music and drawing. Even when Joachim and Lucas would come to fetch her to go surfing, like they do every day of every summer, she preferred to stay shut away. This fresh start is full of promise, I want to believe in it with her. I sprawl beside her, swipe a handful of her snacks, and watch Rachel announcing to Ross that she's pregnant.

E mma is sleeping at Alex's more and more often. She always offers to stay with me, but I make out that I don't need her to. The truth is that I've never lived alone, and I don't like it.

I arrive at the shelter as it's opening. My internship at a special-needs school ended yesterday. I spent six weeks with children with autistic spectrum disorder, and it reinforced what I was thinking: I'm made for looking after others. I'm back in class on Monday, so I'm going to take advantage of the three-day weekend to welcome my new companion.

The barking breaks my heart. As I walk along the aisles, I resist the temptation to open the cages and free all the dogs.

When Dad died, I convinced myself that Mom was right to return Snoopy to a shelter. For ages, it stopped me from sleeping, I'd imagine him alone, wondering why he didn't see us anymore, I'd ask heaven for someone to send him some new owners.

I notice a splendid Labrador; he licks my hand through the bars. The label says he's called Sultan and is three years old. His cellmate joins us. I didn't know that much ugliness could be combined in a single creature. Nothing's right with this animal, it's as if all the elements were thrown together randomly. He's a canine Mr. Potato Head. The label says he's called Joey and is eight years old. He hangs back, seemingly indifferent to my presence.

When Emma gets in, I hear her screech before I see her:
"What's that?"
"I reckon it's a dog, but I don't want to stick my neck out."
The mutt is lying on his back on the sitting-room carpet.

"But what the hell's it doing there?"

"I adopted him."

"What? But Agathe, have you lost the plot? Who's going to look after it? We're away all day, is it just going to be left on its own?"

"He'll still be better off than at the shelter. He's eight years old and looks like a porcupine, no one would have wanted him. D'you know, he'd been there for three years?"

She looks at him. He wags his tail.

"You see, he's a metronome, too. I couldn't not take him."

She crouches down, sighing, the dog gets up and comes over to spread hairs on her black trousers.

"In any case, I've got no choice. What's it called?"

"Mr. Potato Head. Mr. Potato Head Delorme."

11:40 A.M.

"So, good massage?" I ask Agathe.

"I can't tell you, I wasn't massaged, I was dug over."

"Your masseuse wasn't gentle?"

"Gentleness personified. Like Mom when she's plastered."

It's supposed to be funny, but the joke falls flat.

"Truthfully, it did me good," Agathe backtracks. "Thanks for the surprise."

She slaps a kiss on my cheek and takes a plastic sachet out of her bag:

"I pinched a disposable G-string. As a souvenir."

12:02 P.M.

I spend the car journey shifting noisily in my seat, in case another spider decides to show up. Papi taught me that, when I was little, when we were looking for porcini in the forest: "You must make a noise as you walk, it keeps snakes away."

"Got ants in your pants?" Agathe asks.

I smile at hearing that old expression of our parents.

My sister reaches over and turns up the volume. Céline Dion's voice fills the car.

"Remember?" she asks me.

"You bet I remember."

When I dragged my sister to the cinema to see *Titanic*, she came reluctantly. I'd already seen it five times there and had cried almost the equivalent of the entire North Atlantic. I talked about it non-stop, I was devastated by this tragic tale, and obsessed with the love story of Rose and Jack. I longed for just one thing: to love, one day, just as intensely. In my fervor, I'd told the ending to Agathe, who couldn't see the point of watching the movie anymore. As we left the cinema, she asked me when we'd be coming back. She was hooked. We saw it again the following week, then the one after that, and the one after that. Each time we emerged red-eyed and runny-nosed. The cashier at the cinema ended up taking pity and would let us in for free.

A few months later, on the day the CD of the original soundtrack was released, I bought it. We listened to it on repeat for weeks. I can still see us, sitting on my bed, translating the lyrics in the songbook with an English-French dictionary, to understand what Céline Dion was saying, with results that were approximate, to say the least.

The words "You're safe" we translated into "*Tu es coffre*"— "You're a safe"—and no one reacted.

We haven't forgotten the words. In the car, we sing at the top of our voices, with the windows open. People look around as we pass, and we couldn't care less. We're back in our teen bedroom with Rose and Jack.

"You know that Jack could have lived?" Agathe suddenly asks me. "There was ample space for two on that door, it's been proven by experts."

"Stop it. I've been told that before, but I refuse to accept the theory."

"Why?"

"Because it would change my image of Rose, and no one touches Rose DeWitt Bukater."

"Okay, so we don't mention the fact that she leaves Jack handcuffed for hours before realizing that he's the victim of a plot?"

"We don't."

"Right. Nothing about the priceless necklace thrown to the bottom of the sea?"

"I'm not listening to you. Youuuu're heeeeere, theeere's nooooothing I fear."

12:23 P.M.

We looked in Mima's recipe notebook and decided to make pasta with zucchini. It's not complicated, everything rests on how the zucchini are cooked. They must be lightly grilled on the outside and soft inside. Agathe sees to the chopping, while I grate the Parmesan.

"Mom called," she suddenly says.

"Oh."

"She asked if she could come by. She'd like to see you."

I rub the cheese furiously against the grater.

"You know I don't want to see her anymore."

"I do know. But she's getting on, she isn't immortal. You don't want to have regrets one day."

"I didn't know you were talking to her again."

"I never really managed to cut her off. She's my mother."

"She's mine, too. I hate the reproachful tone I can hear in your voice."

She puts the knife down (which suits me) and fixes her eyes on mine:

"No reproach, Emma. I just think that, sometimes, one has to let things go. To be honest, there's worse than her. She's not as terrible as all that."

I open my mouth to respond, to remind her of the almighty beatings, the fits of rage, the objects smashed against the wall, the threats of suicide, the reproaches, but I change my mind. We lived in the same apartment, with the same mother, and yet Agathe and I don't have the same memories, and that's exactly what I'd hoped for. As soon as I could, I used to isolate her in her room, with the music on loud enough to cover the shouting. Sadly, she didn't escape all of it; sometimes, when our mother's anger was directed at her, I didn't manage to divert it onto myself. But compared with mine, her childhood was a little gentler.

"How long's it been since you saw her last?" Agathe asks.

"Seven years. The last time was for my son's third birthday."

"I remember."

She leaves a silence, while dropping the zucchini into the oil, then:

"Have you ever raised a hand to you children?"

"Never. But it does require an enormous effort on my part. Sometimes, my stomach churns with anger, my blood boils in my veins. When they answer back, when I've already repeated something three times, when we're running late. I do occasionally shout. If I let instinct take over, I think I could hit them. But I fight against it. I refuse for my children to quake in front of me as we did in front of Mom. I refuse to be like her. I resent her for this legacy, which obliges me to be in control so as not to give in to my impulses. I resent her for having damaged us."

Agathe stirs the rounds of zucchini in the pan.

"I don't want children," she suddenly says.

"Oh really? But . . . never?"

She laughs:

"When I'm ninety, I'll think about it. But before then, it's a no."

"But why?

"I'm going to answer because it's you, but I have to say: I find having to justify myself intolerable. Women can't declare that they don't want children without having to explain their choice. I don't necessarily need a reason! I don't feel like having any, for a start. It doesn't appeal to me. I've never gone gooey in front of a baby, never dreamed of having a large family, all that stuff. On top of that, to be honest, I'm not sure I'd want to bring someone into this world. I mean, between the climate, the wars, the violence, the poverty, the viruses, and the rest of it, if I'd had the choice, I don't think I'd have poked my own head through the hole. And, mainly, because I'm not like you. When my temper rises, try as

I might, I can't contain it. I wouldn't be a good mother. But, if you'll have me, I can be a good aunt."

I'm stunned by these admissions. I'd never even considered it; for me, it was obvious that Agathe would have children. This formula is so fixed in my mind that I didn't question it, as if the intention of every human being is to reproduce. I pour some water into a saucepan and place it on the ring:

"I will have you, but you must promise me something."

"What?"

"Never tell them that stuff about Rose and Jack."

I jumped on a train to go spend my short vacation with Mima. Since starting my studies, I haven't seen her often enough. For two weeks, I gorged myself on her and her lasagna, and I'm now heading back having gained two kilos and tons of love.

On the return train, with Mr. Potato Head at my feet, I stroke the pearl necklace that I've wound around my wrist, and I struggle not to cry. I gaze out at the scenery, flashing by as fast as time. The days accumulate, become months, years. We go through life at full tilt, all the while telling ourselves we must slow down, but it's time that takes us with it. As soon as we've said it, it's become yesterday. Throughout my childhood, I'd hear, "How she's grown, it goes by so fast." To my ears, it was a hackneyed comment, an adult comment, its only point being to fill the silence. It goes by so fast. It has a different ring to it, now that I'm feeling it. I'd like to freeze time. To remain "the little one." Lock Mima into my life. Share the sofa-bed with Emma forever. If I can do that without having to get them both stuffed, that would suit me fine.

Emma warned me that she'd be at Alex's when I got back, and yet I find her at the studio. I'm about to fly into her arms, but then notice she's crying.

"What's up, Emma?"

"He left me."

She explains that it happened three days ago. She didn't tell me so as not to spoil my vacation.

"He says we're too young to be an old couple, he needs air, he feels stifled."

"It's about time he realized that."

The sentence came out too fast. Emma is now in floods of tears.

"Perhaps it might sort itself out?"

She wipes her nose on her sleeve:

"No, he seems sure. I asked him if he still loved me, he didn't answer."

"What a dork."

"I don't know how I'll get over it. I love him so much . . . I have to go and fetch my things from his place, I couldn't face it."

"Come along, let's go."

"Now?"

"Now."

I fucked up at her last split. I invented my friend Sonia, whom I had to console, when in reality, I panicked, I'd never seen Emma so fragile. She's always been the steady one, the one who takes control of situations and makes decisions. I felt overwhelmed by her suffering, preferred to run away than see my pillar collapsing. I'm determined to make up for that.

Alex isn't there, Emma has the keys. I go in with her. While she gathers the few belongings she left at his studio, I check out the place. Small, light, in a total mess (leftover hamburger and some cold fries languish on the table) (nothing more gross than cold fries). Photos of my sister and Alex hang on the wall. In one, Emma looks straight at the camera, I can see in her eyes that she's happy. It's a shame, him I did rather like.

I hear my sister sobbing in the bathroom. I need to distract her.

When she emerges, her eyes red, she discovers my work. I'm not sure I'm proud of it, it's junior-high level, but it has the merit of making her laugh. With the black marker I always carry around in my bag, I've written on the wall—in very big letters—the first insult that came to me:

YOU FUCKING COLD FRY

O nce again, Agathe has moved all the furniture around. It's the third time this year, and much as I've explained to her that I don't like change, she can't stop herself. Okay, so I do spend two nights a week at Alex's, but it's my home, too.

"Look, this way you can see the sky from the sofa-bed!" she says to convince me.

I lie down beside her, the stars twinkle directly above our heads.

"You see? It's wonderful!"

"I'll give you that, Agathe, but now we can't open the bathroom door."

"You're so pernickety."

I give up, she'll change everything around again when her bladder's bursting.

I try to ignore the drawbacks of cohabitation by thinking that, one day, I'll look back on this period with nostalgia. Most of the time, we get on well. We laugh a lot, we share TV'n'duvet nights, we take care of each other. I have loads of faults, I readily admit. But Agathe is exhausting. I feel like I'm on a roller coaster. She swings from all to nothing, knows no in-between. She goes around with all her emotions on display, and anyone spending time with her has to get used to it. You just have to go with her, on her real highs, on her real lows. Lately, she has a new obsession: writing a comic strip. She devotes all her free time to it, spends all her money and some of mine on notebooks, felt pens and how-to books. She always manages to infect me with her enthusiasm, so I encourage her, listen to her talking about it for hours, but deep down, I fear her passion will end up evaporating, just as it did with Jean Paul Gaultier, tattoos, and watercolors.

There's a knock on the door.

"I'll go!" Agathe cries, diving towards it.

Our mother stands in the doorway.

"Hello, girls. I'm so sorry to come without warning, but I can't take living without you anymore. If you don't want to see me, I can go."

Agathe looks questioningly at me. I don't react at all. We haven't seen our mother since we left her apartment. She hasn't tried to contact us for two years, and now here she is, out of the blue, expecting us to welcome her with open arms.

"How did you know where we live?"

My tone is curter than I'd have wished. Agathe ushers her in, Mr. Potato Head gives her a warm welcome. She crouches to stroke him:

"Your sister gave me the address."

That sister avoids my gaze.

My mother's patchouli scent fills the studio. My stomach is in knots. Her hair is short, her hands shake a little. I'd like to be angry enough to throw her out, not to feel her distress. But in reality, it upsets me to see her so vulnerable. The moment she stands up, when she stops focusing on the dog to avoid facing her girls, I'm in her arms.

3:17 P.M.

She's having a nap. Clearly, her massage really was relaxing. Mine revealed parts of my body I wasn't aware of, and would have gladly remained unaware of. I'm trying to find a suitable position in the armchair to doze off when the doorbell rings. Emma springs up, eyes still sleepy:

"Yes? What?"

I burst out laughing:

"That's good, you're completely relaxed."

I go to open the door while she comes to. A man stands behind the gate. He has white hair and a cat in his arms.

"Robert Redford!"

I invite the man in. He pushes open the gate and joins me. The cat doesn't even look at me. If he could unscrew his head to show his lack of interest, he would.

"I saw the posters," the man says. "Seems you're looking for him."

"Yes, he's my grandmother's cat."

"I know. We were friends."

The words of Madame Garcia, the neighbor, come back to me. She'd mentioned another neighbor Mima was close to. Instantly, the way he speaks of her makes me like him. I usher him inside. Emma is now totally awake; the same cannot be said of her hair.

"He was a friend of Mima's," I tell my sister. "What's your name?"

"Georges Rochefort. I live at no. 14."

Emma offers him a coffee, which he accepts. I suspect that, like me, she wants to hear this man talk about our grandmother. Bring her to life through his words.

With the cat on his knees, Georges Rochefort drops half a sugar lump into his coffee.

"Did you know Mima for a long time?" Emma asks.

"For twenty years."

I hide my surprise, I've never heard mention of him.

"Did you know each other well?"

He smiles:

"We were good friends, yes."

Suddenly, a memory hits me. At Mima's funeral, one man had struck me as particularly upset. I hadn't dwelt on it, too choked up with my own grief, but it had touched me. I wasn't the only one sobbing noisily. He was wearing a hat, but I think I recognize him.

"I've come to ask you if I might keep Robert Redford," Georges says while stroking the cat, who hasn't moved from his knees. "We were on our way to the Quintaou market when we found this cat, injured by a c—"

"You were together?" I ask, surprised.

The story of Robert Redford's rescue, told to me by Mima, is taking on a new shape.

"We always went to the market together."

Emma gives me a knowing look. I can't believe it.

"We had what might be called shared custody," the man jokes. "The cat would come and go between our two houses. He'd spend the day at mine and, once it was evening, he'd return to your grandmother. While she was in hospital, he stayed at mine one night, then a second. I told her about it by phone. She grumbled, fearing he'd abandon her. I promised her that he'd be back as soon as she got home."

He breaks off, looks away. His grief his palpable. Discreetly, Emma forms a heart with her fingers. I shake my head. Mima wasn't attached, I'd have known about it.

"You can keep the cat," Emma says. "We'll take down the posters."

"It's nice that he's with you," I add. "I have a small question, Georges. Did you see each other often, you and Mima?"

His eyes light up, he smiles broadly:

"As often as possible, yes. We liked being together . . . I miss her dreadfully."

He lowers his head, seems to hesitate, then takes a deep breath:

"I have something else to ask you. It's a rather delicate matter, but I'm sure you'll understand."

We look around our studio one last time and then close the door for good.

"It was really lovely living with you," Agathe murmurs.

I wrap my arms around her. She's the only person I can do that to.

I got my degree, she got hers. In September, I'll start my teaching diploma—it's always been my dream. She's off to live with Mima, there's an opening for a youth worker in a home.

The car is loaded to the max. Alex really helped us, he's a Tetris champion. When I'm back, I'll move in with him. I played hard to get for a while. I wanted to be sure he had no more doubts, after his meltdown. He was soon back, he'd been scared, but then realized that he didn't want to live without me.

"Drive carefully," he says, slamming my door shut.

"Don't worry about us, Cold Fry!" Agathe says back.

In the car, we listen to RTL. It's very easy to pinpoint the moment one enters adulthood: it's when one switches from music radio stations to general-interest ones.

We arrive in the dark. Mima welcomes us with a potato omelet, which we devour as if we've not eaten for months. We postpone dealing with Agathe's boxes until tomorrow, preferring to get started on a game of Chinese checkers, which Mima wins, in keeping with tradition, since she bends the rules and we don't dare tell her we've noticed, and then we all retire to our rooms. I inherit my father's old room, as usual, and Agathe gets Uncle Jean-Yves's.

I'm half-asleep when the door opens and I sense my little sister sliding into my bed.

D ecember is my favorite month, here. The tourists have
gone; rock, sky, and sea become one; and, especially:
Christmas is coming. Every year, I wait, like a kid, for the
decorations, and rush to the stores to look for the perfect gifts for
those I love. I've found a splendid scarf for Mima. She had her thy-
roid removed last month and won't go out anymore without some
accessory to hide her neck.

In the warmth of a café, eyes riveted on the illuminations outside, I share a chocolate mousse with Joachim.

"It's really good," I say.

"It's you who's good."

I must really love him to put up with such a corny line.

Things got off to a bad start, between us. For a long time, he was
the friendly neighbor with greasy hair, the one I'd go and find when
Lucas wasn't available for surfing but forget the rest of the time.
Over the years, we became friends, but it would never have entered
my mind to fall in love with him.

And then, this summer, bang, head over heels in love. A revela-
tion. He returned to live with his parents after being dumped, and
it was as if, suddenly, I was seeing him. Luckily, he was seeing me,
too, and apparently had been for some time. When I kissed him, he
said, "Aha, thought so!"

We kept our relationship secret for a while. I'd only told Mima
about it because I can't hide a thing from her. Madame Garcia,
Joachim's mother, isn't exactly crazy about me. He confessed that
she called me "the wild girl," just because I don't wear frumpy out-
fits like her. She looks straight out of the granny pages in the 3

Suisses catalogue, so I can see why she'd be rattled. When Lucas heard about us, he had the same reaction as Joachim: "Aha, thought so!" Apparently, I was the last to know, even though I was the chief concern.

We leave the café and head back to my wild-girl's scooter (it's fluorescent pink). On the way, I buy some roast chestnuts and burn my tongue because I can't wait to taste them.

"Want me to kiss it better?" Joachim teases.

I don't say no, he kisses me, I quiver, we jump on the scooter, I run the lights to get home as fast as possible, and then pounce on him.

It's my longest relationship. It'll be six months next month. I know he's the one, and this time, even Emma doesn't tell me otherwise. She's clearly seen that it's different.

He's the first person I've found a gift for. For Christmas, I'm giving him a life with me.

3:45 P.M.

Georges Rochefort is waiting for us at the bottom of the ladder. His request isn't as sensitive as he suggested: he'd like to recover a painting, done by a Spanish artist for Mima and him, about fifteen years ago. All perfectly reasonable, in fact.

"It's surprising she didn't hang it up!" Agathe says.

"The painting is rather unusual," Georges replies. "It doesn't fit in easily with the décor."

Agathe and I had no idea the house even had an attic. Georges showed us the trapdoor to access it (in the utility room, just above the water-heater), and the location of the ladder (in the garage). Brave as ever, Agathe lets me climb up first.

"I saw a movie about a guy living in an attic for years without the homeowner realizing," she says. "If you see someone, shout 'Danger!', and I'll understand."

"Are you sure about that?"

I push the trapdoor, it doesn't give.

"Must have been closed for a long time," I say.

"That's reassuring," Agathe says. "If there *is* a squatter, he'll be dead by now."

I think I hear Georges chuckling. The trapdoor finally opens, and I hoist myself into the attic.

"You can come now, Agathe!"

"Are you sure? No one on the horizon?"

"The man holding the gun to my temple is ordering me to tell you there's no one."

"Ha ha, very funny . . . You're joking, aren't you?"

She finally joins me. A small dormer window lets some light in. The attic extends right across the house, which isn't huge, and, to my great surprise, it's all fitted out. The floor is carpeted, the walls papered. Shelves are groaning with all manner of things: plates, books, folded clothes, a toaster, shoes, an electric whisk, cushions, a carafe, porcelain figures, sheets, curtains, Christmas baubles, strings of lights, a mirror, some perfume miniatures. I recognize the twenty-two-volume encyclopedia in which Papi would find the answer to all the questions we asked him, the electric razor he used every morning in the bathroom, his carpet slippers.

"Come and see this," Agathe says, in front of an open chest.

We understand without having to rummage. Dad's belongings are stored here. His school exercise books, a wooden train, his watch, his checked shirts, his scent. Scorpio. I'd given him a bottle one Father's Day, my mother had steered me to it because it wasn't expensive, it was sold in the supermarket. He'd stuck with it and wore it on special occasions. Agathe grabs the red bottle and presses the atomizer. The fragrance enters my nostrils and brings my father back to me. Just for a second, he's there, in front of me, his broad shoulders, his moustache, his smile, his voice. Agathe's hand slips into mine.

Further along, we fall on my Speak & Spell and Agathe's firefly. Our slot-in record player is there, too, beside a Popple toy.

In her notebook of poems, Mima often wrote about time passing. One poem, dating to the year of my birth, is imprinted on my memory.

It's over there that my father now lives
There, too, that Mom went
I left my little ones' laughter there
And my youthful years remained there
Our first dance disappeared there
I turn around, but I see them no more

If only for one moment I could
Freeze time and find Yesterday again.

It isn't an attic, it's a mausoleum. Mima preserved her passing time here.

"Have you found it?" asks Georges.

"I'd forgotten about him," Agathe mutters.

"Not yet!" I answer. "Do you remember where you put it?"

"It was to the right. Near a barrel, I think."

Agathe shows me the barrel, made by Papi, at the back of the room. We make our way over, stooping due to the sloping roof. The painting is there, facing the wall. I grab it and turn it around.

"Oh my god!" I exclaim.

"Not an improvement," Agathe says, covering her eyes.

Georges didn't lie, it sure is an unusual painting. A portrait of him and Mima, to be precise. Smiling, neatly coifed, and stark naked.

9:32 P.M.

He answers at the first ring.

"Hi, sweetheart."

Hi, sweetie. How are you doing?"

"Fine. I'm missing you."

"I'm pleased to hear it."

"I'm pleased to feel it."

Silence.

"Are you annoyed with me?"

"It isn't easy, I can't deny it. I've definitely felt that you've been distant lately."

"I'm really sorry."

"Don't worry, I understand. With all that's happened, you've every right to be shaken up."

"No doubt. But so have you."

From his voice, I can tell he's choking up.

"Let's just say we're quits. Remember, at the start of our relationship, it was me who needed air."

"True. I hope, when I get home, I won't find anything scrawled on the wall."

He laughs.

"Promise. I leave that privilege to your sister. How's it going, with her?"

"Well. Very well, even. It's good to have her back."

"I'm happy for you."

"How are the children?"

"They come back exhausted from the outdoor center, they enjoy it. They can't wait for you to come home. Alice is doing lots of drawings for you, we won't have enough walls to hang them all up."

I laugh:

"Don't throw a single one away!"

"Oh no, I wouldn't dare! I know you're going to keep them, even those that are just a squiggle."

I laugh. He knows me perfectly.

"You know, the other evening I realized that it'll soon be twenty years, can you imagine? We've almost spent as much time together as apart."

He coughs, like whenever he's emotional. I feel sadness sweep through me, a massive wave. The floodgates are about to open, I must about-turn.

"I have to go now, sweetheart. Agathe's waiting for me to play Chinese checkers."

"Go easy on the verbena tea."

"I prefer shots of lime-blossom. I know, I'm a punk."

"I love you, my punk."

"I love you too."

"Emma?"

"Yes?"

"Have you done it?"

"Not yet. Soon."

Mr. Potato Head has died. He waited for me, I'm sure of it. He wasn't looking great when I left for work. He was dragging during our walk this morning, and he usually trots from one tree to another, sniffing away and wagging his tail as if he was a puppy. I'd forgotten that he was old. When we got back, he headed straight to the cupboard for his daily treat, then settled in his big basket beside Mima, who was reading in her armchair.

I'd just returned from my lunch break when she called me to say he was in a bad way. My spud wasn't getting up anymore and was breathing very rapidly. I went into automatic pilot, jumped on my scooter, and rode home. He took his last breath in my arms.

I'm devastated.

Images from the past three years flood my mind like a slide show.

We call animals our companions, and for good reason. Mr. Potato Head was an extension of me, the sound of his paws on the floor accompanied me everywhere, he sensed how I was feeling, sometimes before I was aware of it myself. When I was sad, he'd lay his head on my thigh, and the love I read in his eyes, that unconditional and unjudgmental love that only animals can give, would console me a little. I didn't know you could love an animal more fiercely than you love humans. He's here, in my arms, still warm, but already gone. This time he won't console me. I feel dizzy.

Mima hugs me. She holds in her grief, leaving all the space to mine. And yet I know how much she, too, loved Mr. Potato Head's company. It was with her that he'd stay all day long. She knitted him a sweater for cold days, and, despite my forbidding it, she'd often tip our leftovers into his bowl.

I don't know how I'm going to manage without him.

I call Emma, I need to talk to her, as I do whenever I'm un-happy. I get the answering machine, she must be at work. I leave her a message.

We stay there for a while, an hour maybe, not really knowing what to do. In a daze.

"Would you like us to go to the vet?" Mima suggests. "I believe it's he who takes care of what comes next."

She doesn't say the word. Cremation. It's the kind of word one says in a hushed voice, or hides behind three little dots.

"Can we bury him in the garden?"

A sob takes my breath away.

"Mr. Potato Head will rest beside the hydrangeas," Mima replies.

I smile. She was forever battling with him to stop lifting his leg on her hydrangeas.

Mima informs me that quicklime must be poured into the hole before covering it over. I go off to buy some, making her promise not to start digging. When I go back to my scooter on the sidewalk, I see Joachim's car parked outside his house. I thought he was at work, didn't want to disturb him, but he's here, his arms are here, his lips are here, his voice is here, he'll hold me tight and put all the scattered pieces of me back together again.

I open the gate, his parents are at work at this time, and there's no chance of my being bitten by his mother. I knock on the door, no one answers. I walk around the house, peer through the windows. My face is haggard from crying. I've never needed him more. I find him in his bedroom. Our eyes meet through the glass. I don't know what he sees in mine, but I can clearly make out what his say: "Shit, I've just been caught screwing another woman."

There are two messages on my phone when I leave the pool.

I don't listen to them immediately. First I call the teacher of my teacher-training class, then I call Alex.

"I'll be back a bit later, sweetheart. I've got some shopping to do. Anything you need?"

"Oh, yes!" he replies. "I've run out of yogurt, could you get some?"

"Vanilla, right?"

"Right. See you later, sweetie. Hey, it was nice, this morning . . ."

I haven't dried my hair, and water is dripping down my back. It's mild for late October, but I'm shivering.

I buy everything on my list. Dried goods first, then produce, ending with frozen. I'm at the till when I realize I've forgotten the coffee. For a moment, I consider carrying on as if I hadn't thought of it. If I go back now, I'll lose my place in the line, it's busy as hell, I want to get home. But I know how much Alex loves his coffee. I leave the line and push the caddy to the breakfast section.

I'm holding two packs when my phone rings. I can't remember which he prefers, strong or mild. I put back the mild and answer.

It's Mima. I have to make her repeat what she's saying several times, I can't understand a word. It sounds like she's crying. She takes a breath and manages to articulate:

"Darling, your sister's in hospital. She did something silly."

The strong coffee falls with a thud at my feet.

7:52 A.M.

There's not a single wave. The sea is dozing, smooth as a lake. I cleave through the water in slow motion, trying not to cause the slightest ripple. The water is limpid: submerged up to my shoulders, I can still see my feet. My toes sink into the sand. The beach is deserted, but, in the distance, near the Rock of the Virgin, I can just see an early morning swimmer. I lift my feet from the bottom and start doing breast-stroke. The water slides over my body, I dip my head in, lift it out, take a breath. I move towards the open sea without looking back. Every Tuesday morning, at the local pool, I swim length after length without stopping. I get there as it opens, when the pool isn't busy, and, stroke after stroke, I leave my pains and anxieties behind. But I'd forgotten how much the sea, its eddies, its vastness, its mystery, its salty taste, its danger perhaps, made me feel fully alive.

I've just passed the arched rock when I'm stopped by a cramp in my calf. I stretch the leg out, extend my foot, but the pain persists, I'm incapable of swimming. Panic takes over, I'm out of breath, I look around for a solution. On the beach, the seagull man has just arrived. I sometimes imagine my death, but ending up as fish and bird food has never occurred to me. I tip backwards, stretch out my body, and let it float. I close my eyes and focus on my breathing, on the sensation of the cool water on my skin. Little by little, my entire body relaxes. I can feel it distinctly, centimeter by centimeter. The toes first, the legs becoming lighter, the gentle lapping on my fingers, the sun's caress on my face, my back unknotting, my breathing slowing, my thoughts quietening, the silence in my ears. Immersed in the elements, weightless, each cell of my body tuned in, I feel alive. An integral part of the great whole, which was there before me and will continue after me. Ephemeral and eternal. A tear slips between my lashes and rolls down my cheek, before returning to the sea.

8:12 A.M.

I take my time getting back to the beach.

I idealized this week. In the days leading up to it, to allay my fears, I convinced myself it was going to be perfect. It isn't. It's better than that. It's crammed with shortcomings, unawkward silences, raucous laughter. This week resembles us as much as it brings us together. I get Agathe back, but not exactly to where I'd left her. She's true to herself, fiery and extreme, but I sense she's more assured, as if she's emerged from thick fog. For five years, we lived in the first person. In a heartbeat, we'd left our shared path to advance along parallel routes. This five-year deviation brought us back together. We could have changed, not recognized each other, or not have changed at all, and not been able to tolerate each other anymore, but it took less than a minute to set off again, side by side. There's something between us that's stronger than all the arguments, more resistant than all the differences, I can feel it now, and feel stronger for it.

There's a light breeze as I come out of the water. I run to my things to wrap myself in my towel. Seagull man, his feet planted on the wet sand, throws food into the water. I greet him with a nod.

"Piss off, you jerk!" he replies.

While I dry myself, I wonder why this man aggressively rejects human interaction. Maybe he's unhappy and thinks he's protecting himself. Or has only experienced difficulties with the people he's met. I'd like to show him that not everyone wishes him ill, that one can be polite and friendly without expecting anything in return, without seeking to offend him. I slip on my dress and walk over to him, convinced that going gently, finding the right words is all that's needed.

"Monsieur, I admire you for coming to feed the seagulls every morning."

He doesn't take his eyes from the horizon and continues to throw handfuls of food to the birds. Up close, I see that it's shrimps and small fish. Nothing indicates that he's heard me. I persist:

"Apparently, you've been doing so for a long time?"

He turns his head slowly towards me and stares at me. The gulls wheel around us, screeching. His eyes are an almost translucent blue and his skin is abnormally smooth. I smile and repeat my question:

"Have you been doing so for a long time?"

He plunges his hand into his bag, brings it out full of crustaceans, and flings them in my face:

"Did nature make you so stupid or do you take evening classes?"

T omorrow's Christmas Day, and I got my present early: Agathe's leaving the clinic.

The doctors took good care of her. They say she's suffering from depression and an anxiety disorder. They prescribed her medication and she'll undergo therapy.

She promised me she didn't want to die anymore.

It took a long time. When she came around, after doing "something silly," she regretted having bungled it.

Writing on walls with a marker pen, that's "silly." Breaking a glass, that's "silly." Cutting one's own fringe, that's "silly." But swallowing two boxes of tranquillizers, that's called a suicide attempt.

Mima never could say those words, she prefers to gloss over them. She found Agathe inert in her bed, thought she was dead, had to leave her on her own, get to the phone to call the emergency services, wait seemingly endless minutes; she saw the ambulance arriving, the men entering her house, trying to rouse her granddaughter, taking her away, and, without knowing if she'd see her again, she had to follow them at the wheel of her car, halt at stop signs, not jump the lights, find a space in the packed car park, sit on the plastic chair, stare at the clock on the white wall, banishing dark thoughts, jumping each time the door opened, negotiating silently with God, realizing she hadn't taken off her slippers; had to hear a doctor telling her they'd had to pump Agathe's stomach, that she'd pulled through, that she'd have to go to a clinic. She must have wondered a thousand times why Agathe had done that. Whether she could have done anything at all to stop her. So, if she wants to call it "something silly," I'm certainly not going to stop her.

Agathe is waiting for me in her room. She had to be collected, they wouldn't let her go out alone. Her bag is ready, she's already got her coat on. She throws herself into my arms. I've not seen her since she was admitted. She'd phone me every day but preferred not to be visited. I bury my face in her curls, and behind the smell of the clinic is that of my little sister. I promised myself not to cry, so as not to spoil this moment of joy, but the floodgates open. I'd been so very scared. In fact, I've never been so terrified in my life. I came close to losing her, glimpsed the outline of a world without her. Even on the threshold of that loss, it was already unbreathable. I didn't dare imagine what actually entering it would be like.

I don't ask her a single question, and yet I've had hundreds in my head since she did what she did. All that matters is that she's here. Standing. Alive.

I'm dying to discover her reasons, to know whether she'd already thought about doing it, whether it was impulsive. Whether she couldn't bear living anymore or wanted to die. Whether she wanted to quit suffering or quit life. The subtle difference is massive. I can't stop thinking of the despair one must feel to reach the point of wanting to stop everything. The pain I feel imagining her distress is sometimes physical. I don't know if having shared the same uterus gives us the power to feel each other's emotions, but one thing's certain: a bond as inexplicable as it is intangible exists between brothers and sisters, the same one that allows us to understand each other with a mere glance, to forgive each other in a second, like a bridge crossed by the senses, a bond that tears us to shreds when the other one suffers and thrills us when they're happy.

I throw her bag onto my shoulder, Agathe gives the room a final look, I take her hand, and bring her back into life.

I was bound to run into him one day. He's returning to his parents' house just when I'm going out to buy some cigs.

"Happy Christmas, Agathe."

"Unhappy Christmas, dickhead."

"I tried to call you. Why didn't you answer?"

"I have nothing to say to you."

"I'm really sorry. It's not what you think. I feel nothing for her. It was an accident."

"Sure. What did you write in the accident report? That she inadvertently slipped and impaled herself on your dick?"

"Stop with your cynicism, it meant nothing! It's you I love. She came on to me for weeks, any man would have given in. She knew I had a girlfriend, it must have turned her on."

"Oh, my poor darling! What a terrible witch! She forced you . . . Having said that, she must have got a surprise. You tend to go for it like a pneumatic drill, she must have thought you were looking for oil."

He rolls his eyes:

"That's low."

"You're the expert on that."

"I dare you to tell me you don't love me anymore."

"I love the guy I thought I knew. Not the coward in front of me."

"Give us a chance. Don't be so categorical. There are plenty of couples who survive a bit on the side."

He gets down on one knee.

"Agathe, will you be my wife?"

"Get up, Joachim. Your dignity's on the floor."

He gets up.

"I thought you'd be mature enough for us to get over this together . . . "

"You chose to fuck around, I wasn't part of the plan, so we're not getting over anything together."

"This is exactly why I looked elsewhere. You're hard, Agathe, there's a wall between you and the rest of the world. I did everything to knock it down, but you let no one in."

"Okay, Joachim, I've got to go."

"You see, you run away. As usual."

I head for my scooter. He catches up with me:

"And don't make out that you did what you did because of me. I won't be blamed for you going to hospital. It's something you'd have ended up doing anyway. You and I know that it goes deeper than that."

"Right, mate. All the best."

"One last thing: I'm moving next week, I found an apartment. You should be pleased, we won't see each other anymore. Until then, could you tell your sister to stop scratching my car? I've seen her, she's hardly discreet."

I turn right around, cross the garden, open the door, rejoin Emma in the sitting room, and give her the biggest hug.

9:03 A.M.

I get up at the first ring of the alarm clock. I want to relish our last two days. I open the shutters, the sun takes its chance to blithely burn my eyes. I don't like the heat. Having said that, I don't like the cold, either, but it has a not inconsiderable advantage: you can cover yourself up, pile on sweaters, jackets, scarves to forget about it. When it's too hot, all you can do is go naked, and even then, that's not acceptable everywhere. The result: I drag myself around and I sweat. Much to my despair, my sweat isn't like that on the ads, a light moistness one can mask with vanilla-scented deodorant. No, my sweat can strip wallpaper. I'd like to live forever in autumn or spring (or be fitted with an internal thermostat.)

I walk down the stairs, the house is silent. Emma must have gone for a swim. I put the coffee on and toast two slices of bread, get out the butter (with actual salt crystals) and the strawberry jam. When I was little, Mima would make me something for breakfast that only I liked. She'd beat egg yolks and caster sugar over a bain-marie until the mixture became lightly frothy. She'd explained to me that it was an alcohol-free version of an Italian recipe, zabaglione, which normally accompanies cakes or fruit. As for me, I'd gobble it up by the spoonful, then lick the bowl.

I'm just loading everything onto a tray when I hear a noise from the garden. I look out of the window: a man is standing near the swing seat. He's looking towards the house. Bravely, I dive to the floor and end up flat on my stomach. It's always the same, fear gives orders to my body without checking with my brain. I can hear my heart pounding in my ears and I'm quaking at 7 on the

Richter scale. The alarm's been turned off and my phone's still in my room. I have to get up there somehow, but first, I must find a weapon. It won't be said that Agathe Delorme capitulated without a fight. I seize the first thing that comes to hand. It happens to be a butter knife, my luck has clearly remained upstairs with my phone, but I don't have time to look for anything better. I hear the man approaching. I crawl towards the stairs. In my head, I'm John Rambo; in reality, I'm an elephant seal. Once at the bottom of the stairs, I can hear voices. A woman is talking to him. I have no chance against two assailants. I crouch and am about to go upstairs when a head appears, pressed to the smoked glass of the front door.

"AAAAAAAAAAAAAAAARGH!"

"Anyone there?" the voice asks.

"NO!" I scream.

"Could you open up please? We're the new owners."

"Prove it!"

I hear the woman cackling. The man tries to convince me:

"We found the property through the 5 Cantons real-estate agency, the seller is called Jean-Yves Delorme, we signed the sales agreement with the lawyer named Etcheverry."

I open the door, still gripping the butter knife. They're young, early thirties. The woman holds out her hand to me:

"Marie Louillet, how do you do?"

"Michaël Louillet," her husband says, shaking my hand in turn. "We're awfully sorry, we thought no one would be here. We just need to take a few measurements in the garden for the swimming pool. We mustn't get it wrong, there are local planning-office restrictions, or we can be made to demolish it. Did you rent the place for a vacation?"

"I'm the granddaughter of the owner. Well, the former owner. Agathe Delorme."

"Oh, I'm so sorry," the woman goes. "I lost my grandmother recently, I know how hard it is. By the way, we don't want to bother you, but since you're here, would it be possible for us to take a few measurements inside? We only get the keys at the end of the month, and I'd like to start buying some furniture."

I open the door wide to let them in. I can't speak. I'm kind of stunned, thrust into a reality I've been trying my best to ignore.

The woman lays her hand on my shoulder as she goes past. The gesture brings tears to my eyes. Comforting gestures are always surer to make me cry than the sorrows themselves.

I observe them from a distance. Tape measure in hand, they check the length of the sitting-room wall, the height above the sink. Snatches of sentences reach me: "It isn't a load-bearing wall, we can knock through it . . . " "It'll be far more spacious without the dresser . . . " "I can just see the TV unit here."

I take refuge in the kitchen and gaze at my toast, which I no longer feel like eating.

"Agathe?"

Emma has just come in. I briefly explain the situation to her.

"They're upstairs, if you want to go and see them."

"Will you come with me?" she asks.

"I don't really want to."

"You should. It'll give you a chance to put some clothes on."

I look down and realize, with horror, that I'm in my undies. She laughs so much, it's infectious. I follow her upstairs and, while she's introducing herself, I slip on a dress.

When I join them, they're measuring the cupboard in Papi's and Mima's room. From a photograph on the bedside table, my grandparents watch us.

"It's my favorite room," Marie Louillet tells us. "It's lovely and light, and you can just see the Pyrenees in the distance. It'll be our child's room."

She strokes her belly:

"You're the first to know, we still haven't told anyone."

"We're going to be happy here," her husband adds, putting his arm around her.

They're sweet, but they're going to end up giving me diabetes.

"I imagine you're attached to this house," she says. "When I went to my grandmother's house for the last time, I thanked each room for the lovely times I'd had in it. I honestly think it helped me to say goodbye to her. Just in case it helps you, too . . . "

"We'll see," I reply. "We're not there yet, we still have two days."

She nods, and they return to their measuring.

10:14 A.M.

Emma closes the door. They've just left.

"A new family will grow up here," she goes. "I like them. I'm sure they'll be happy in this house."

I nod, so as not to leave her hanging, but life has proved to me several times that it's unpredictable. I imagine Mima and Papi, sixty years back, taking the measurements of the rooms to fit their furniture into them. They were around twenty, and sure they'd be happy. They were, most of the time, despite having to endure the deepest grief.

My coffee's cold, I make a fresh one.

"You know what we should do?" Emma says.

"Not yet."

"Pack up some of Mima's things and donate them to a charity."

"You've forgotten that our dear uncle has hired some company to clear the house out."

"I have not forgotten. My plan has three objectives: do something charitable, give a nice second life to Mima's things, and seriously annoy Uncle J-Y."

"You're getting worse than me. I adore you."

11:30 A.M.

We filled three large bags. Each garment pulled on the thread of a memory. The sky-blue dress Mima wore at Emma's wedding. The cream cardigan from when I got back from the clinic. The jeans I made her buy. The royal-blue blouse she always wore. Imagining them on people who need them comforts me a little. I've always been excessively attached to objects. As if they had feelings, I feel bad for them when they're abandoned. When I was six, I dropped, out of the car window, a little figurine I'd got free in a box of detergent. It was of no value, and I wasn't particularly attached to it, and yet imagining it alone on that road, with all those cars driving by, risking been run over at any moment, stopped me from sleeping for an entire night. At fifteen, the scrunchy holding my hair during a surfing lesson slipped off and disappeared into the sea. I cried over it for hours. At twenty, I felt sorry for a little pea left on its own at the bottom of the tin, so I tipped it into the pan where its family was waiting for it. At thirty, there were two toothbrushes left at the drugstore. At first, I chose the pink one, then put it back to take the green one, then realized that it was inhuman to abandon the first one after giving it false hope. Needless to say, they both ended up in my bathroom. My case is already interesting when meaningless objects are involved, it becomes fascinating when those with sentimental value are concerned. Those given to me by people I love, those that belonged to my loved ones, those that remind me of a special time. If I could, I'd keep all of Mima's belongings. I'd keep the house, and put it under a cloche to preserve her smell, her voice, and our memories. But that's impossible.

Never again will I turn into this road or pass this gate.

"We should choose what we want to take away."

"Meaning?" asks my sister, clearly as upset as me at being plunged into the past like this.

"Seeing as the jewelry box is empty, I presume Jean-Yves and his family have already taken what they wanted. The rest will disappear. We, too, have a right to our own mementos."

She considers for a few seconds, I bet she's wondering if it's legal, if it could be held against us.

"You're right," she finally says.

12:54 P.M.
We didn't take much.
The recipe notebook.
The booklet of poems.
Dad's scent.
Papi's cassette recorder.
Some photo albums.
The firefly.
The Popples toy.
Dad's watch.
The slot-in record player.
The royal-blue blouse.

The toilet-paper holder. Papi had made it, out of wood. As you pulled the paper, the holder would make a clunking sound. We always took too much when we were little, so Mima would automatically say to us, through the door: "Easy on the paper!" It had become a game. The holder will take its place in my own bathroom, and every time I use it, I'll hear Mima's voice.

T he other evening, Mima and I came across a program featuring several people who were passionate about baking. It's our little ritual: after supper, we settle in front of the TV. We go for shows we can be cutting about, it makes us laugh. I'll miss those evenings when I'll have my own place. Mima says I can stay as long as I like, but I'll have to fly off one day or another. I didn't tell her, but I've already viewed an apartment in Bayonne. It was small and the only window looked out onto the communal staircase, so I let it go.

I was glued to the screen, mesmerized by the incredible cakes these people were creating. The only time I've baked, it looked more gastroenteritis than gateau.

"It looks easy, like that," Mima said.

"Makes me want to try," I replied.

The following day, I bought a dozen books to learn the basics of bakery. I could see myself in the kitchen, apron tied around waist, plunging my hands into the dough, melting the chocolate, piping the icing, making fondant decorations. I wrote a list of all the equipment I needed to buy. It added up to a small fortune, particularly since Mima's oven wasn't ideal and I'd found the perfect one, fan-assisted and with a pyrolytic self-cleaning system. I checked my bank account, it said "no way," so I called a company that had a full-page ad in the TV listings mag, and took out a loan.

The oven has just been delivered. I found all the cake pans I was looking for, some in silicone. I have enough flour, sugar, and butter to survive a siege. I've replaced all of Mima's saucepans (she said there was no need, like for the oven, but when she sees the result, *she'll tell me I was right,) and invested in a good electric whisk and kneading mixer. The whole loan got spent, and I had to extend it a little, but I'm super excited! I'll spend every weekend and some evenings after work in the kitchen and bake us some lovely cakes. Maybe one day, even, my passion will become something more— one of the amateur bakers on the TV show takes orders for special occasions. I like my work too much to give it up, but perhaps I could combine the two!*

I'm testing the oven's different functions when Emma arrives. She's making the most of the vacation by coming to spend a few days here.

"Oh! You've got a new oven, Mima?"

I explain my plan to her, show her my utensils, my books, tell her about the TV show.

"Agathe, could I just say hello to Mima?"

My enthusiasm crashes to the floor.

"Fine, I was just happy to share my passion with you. But if you're not interested . . ."

"I didn't say that, Agathe. Just let me put my things down and say hello!"

I return to the kitchen while she talks with Mima. I'm offended. Offended and hurt. I'm sure they're talking about me. Emma comes back a few minutes later.

"Come on, Gagathe, tell me all about it."

"No, it's fine."

"Stop sulking! I'm really interested."

"Sure you are."

"Agathe, this is getting really tiresome. If you don't want to tell me about it, I'll go back to the sitting room, I'm not going to beg you."

"Oh no, you'd never lower yourself to that for me."

"Meaning?"

"The tea towels, the napkins, all that."

"For fuck's sake, what are you on about?"

"You know very well, you were always the best out of us two. The one who succeeds at everything, whom everyone likes, who doesn't rock the boat. You're hardly going to lower yourself to try to understand me!"

Emma takes the hit:

"You're being unfair, Agathe."

"You see, even now, you're just leaving me to argue with myself! My feelings are no less important than yours! I always felt like a piece of shit next to you, it's not easy, following in the footsteps of the perfect sister."

"And it's my fault if you feel like that?"

I shrug.

It isn't her fault, it's probably nobody's fault. Maybe it's all part of being the younger sister, taking your older sister as your model and never feeling good enough. Maybe it's due to our differences, to her smoother side, which, by contrast, makes my rough edges stand out. But the fact remains that I often feel like I have to gesticulate and speak louder just to exist.

Emma leaves the kitchen, then suddenly returns:

"You see, I was going to encourage you, tell you what good it would do you to start baking, but I'm going to tell you what I really think: You've bankrupted yourself for nothing, you've totally messed up Mima's kitchen for nothing, because in three days' time, you'll have, once again, moved on to something else."

I don't get time to respond, Mima shows up.

"Girls, you're not going to start! Just stop squabbling, you've only just got together again. Come on, give each other a kiss."

She always did that when we argued as little girls. She'd force us to make up and give each other a kiss. We know it's pointless to resist, she'll end up winning anyhow. So we each step forward and, in turn, give each other a kiss while whispering an insult.

When the bell goes for recess, Chloé asks to speak to me. I wait until all the pupils have left, Matteo dawdles, hoping to listen in, I suspect. I go to the door, he's a few centimeters away, head turned towards the classroom.

"Would you like us to speak loudly, Matteo? So you can hear?"

"Oh, no miss! I couldn't care less, I'm just waiting for Dario."

I close the door, Chloé seems uncomfortable. I know her family circumstances. Divorced parents, lives with the father, along with her little brother, who's eight.

"I couldn't do the homework," she tells me.

"Oh? Did you have a problem?"

She squirms:

"Not really, well, my father has a lot of work this week . . ."

"And that prevents you from doing your homework?"

She hangs her head and seems engrossed in her shoes.

"Chloé, you can tell me everything, you know."

"I have to look after my brother."

She whispered, almost inaudibly. She doesn't dare look at me anymore.

"I watch over his shower, his homework, make supper, and put him to bed. Léo doesn't listen much, it isn't easy."

"Sorry? But you're ten years old! What time does your father get home?"

My reaction surprised her, I must show less emotion.

"Dunno, I'm asleep when he gets in. But it's soon over, just three more days to go!"

"Chloé, may I ask you a question?"

She nods.

"Why don't you go and live with your mother?"

"Oh, I'd really love to! But Léo won't hear of it. He doesn't want to go there anymore, since she came out of prison."

"I didn't know. I'm so sorry . . . And you don't want to go on your own?"

"No way am I abandoning my little brother!"

"I understand, Chloé, but you can't sacrifice yourself for others."

"Miss, you wouldn't understand. He's my brother, and that's that."

She gets up and grabs her bag. I lay my hand on her forearm:

"I understand you more than you think."

4:25 P.M.

I'd wanted to know more about Agathe's work, so she suggested I come with her and see for myself. We ride together on her scooter and turn into a driveway that leads to a large stone building. Beyond it, through the trees, I glimpse the sea.

"It's wonderful!"

"Come, I'll show you the view," Agathe says.

I follow her to the end of a small, wooded garden and discover that we're on top of a cliff overlooking the ocean and the southern Basque coast, right up to Spain.

"I've worked here for three years, and yet I never tire of this," she murmurs.

"You didn't want to work with teenagers anymore?"

"It was becoming too tough. You don't have the means, you feel useless. Even if you support them, many turn out badly. It's depressing, I needed a change."

"So you thought: 'Hey, how about I go and work with people who already have one foot in the grave!'"

She bursts out laughing:

"I admit I was a bit apprehensive, but I really like it. I've become attached to them."

We make our way towards the entrance. Above the door, metal letters read:

The Tamarisks
Residential Care

There's a lady sitting on a bench, in the shade of an oak tree.

"Louise, it's hot, don't you want to go indoors, where it's cool?"

"Oh! Agathe! I didn't see you. Aren't you supposed to be on vacation?"

"I'm just dropping by. I've come to show my sister where I spend my days."

"Pleased to meet you, madame," I say, bowing my head.

"Hello, mademoiselle. You should know that your sister's a treasure! She makes me laugh a lot, and that's all we need, at our age."

Agathe slips her arm under Louise's and accompanies her to the building. Naturally, her pace matches Louise's, her usual energy vanishing for the benefit of her ward. I discover how attentive and gentle she is.

She shows me her office, then a large room full of all sorts: musical instruments, baking utensils (I recognize the silicone molds she'd bought when younger,) fabrics, books, board games.

"This is the special activity hub," she tells me. "Here, every morning, we organize workshops for the residents suffering from cognitive or behavioral disorders. It's important for stimulating them and maintaining social contact. Incredibly, there are some things that never disappear, and they're what we try to find. Take Jean, for example. He's young, barely sixty-nine, but Alzheimer's has already stolen quite a few memories and skills. He almost never speaks, no longer knows how a TV works, needs to be helped with eating, but when I bring out some crossword puzzles and give him the clues, he immediately gives me the solutions. His daughters explained to me that he'd loved doing them, had completed crosswords all his life. So, you see, that has remained. Crazy, hey?"

I listen to her, fascinated, and moved. She's passionate about it.

"Right, come along, it's teatime, they must all be in the communal room."

We walk along several corridors, come across several residents.

Each time, she stops to exchange a few words. She pushes two swing doors and we find ourselves in a large room where around fifty people sit around tables. Louise, the lady we met outside, gives us a little wave. We join her. Beside her, a bright-eyed man observes us.

"Emma, may I introduce Gustave," she coos. "He's my husband."

"Hello, monsieur. Pleased to meet you, my name's Emma, I'm Agathe's sister."

"Hello, how are you, Lise?" he replies.

"My name is Em-ma," I repeat, articulating better.

"Don't bother, it's his favorite joke," Agathe says, laughing away.

Some colleagues come to greet Agathe, a man called Greg, one named Marine. Some residents, too, several waving from a distance or getting up to come over to her.

Right at the back of the room, I notice a man sitting alone at a table, facing away. His shoulder-length white hair reminds me of someone. When he turns his head, I realize it's the old man who feeds the seagulls.

When we leave, I ask Agathe about him.

"Oh, him? That's Léon, a terror. He spends half his time working out how to annoy people, and the other half putting his conclusions into practice. At first, I thought he had some disorder, but the doctors are sure his mind is pretty sound. It's his nature, he's just nasty."

"You know I come across him every morning?"

"Really? Where?"

"You'll see. Tomorrow, I'll take you along with me."

We climb back onto the scooter, she turns on the ignition, and we leave The Tamarisks. If anyone asks, I'll claim it's the wind making my eyes water, but in reality, it's having seen how my sister has finally found her place.

I t's my first time in high heels, and I regret wearing them after the first few steps. I don't know who invented these instruments of torture, but what amazes me most is how everyone else let them get away with it. I kept telling myself that they looked pretty, gave one shapely legs and an elegant walk. I'll have to check, but I'm not sure "elegant" means "like a duck that's just met a shooter." My mother walks beside me, poker-faced.

Alex is already in front of the town hall, surrounded by his parents and friends. Jean-Yves and Geneviève are there, too, Jérôme and Laurent shouldn't be long. In all, around fifty people have come together to celebrate the marriage of Emma and Alex.

My future brother-in-law comes to welcome us.

"Hello, Cold Fry."

"Hello, sister-in-law. Mother-in-law."

He kisses us, and I notice that his lips are trembling.

"Feeling stressed?"

"A bit. It's the first time I'm doing this."

"The last time, too. Otherwise, I'll be obliged to come and tag your face."

"Just for that, I'll stay with her until the end of my days."

He looks at me seriously:

"And you, feeling stressed?"

"A bit. It's the first time I'm doing this, too."

"You are going to make her happy, right?" my mother suddenly asks, in a tone that I dread.

"I promise I'll do all I can."

"Very good. Life hasn't always been gentle with her, you know.

With me neither, in fact. I didn't have much luck, got to say, didn't start with the best hand of cards."

She digs out a handkerchief from her bag and dabs her eyes. Although she's annoying me, I put my hand on her shoulder:

"It's okay, Mom. It's a happy day."

"Oh, I know that! Even if it's not me she's chosen to lead her to her groom."

The mayor saves us from a self-pitying monologue by inviting us to come inside. I stand close to the bridegroom, beside my sister's other witness: her best friend, Margaux. The chairs are arranged on either side of the central aisle, and on each one, a spray of white flowers has been attached.

Emma enters to the sound of Des'ree's "I'm Kissing You," the song from the movie Roméo + Juliet. *God knows how many times we watched that one, swooning at Leonardo DiCaprio's good looks, and crying our hearts out at the end. Luckily, I'd read the play at school, otherwise, once again, she'd have spoilt the ending for me.*

I see her dress for the first time. Despite my attempts, she didn't want to ruin the surprise. Doubtless hoping to crank up the emotional response to her entrance. It's worked. My face is now water-damaged.

On Emma's arm, Mima is splendid in her sky-blue dress. Her eyes are shining, her hands shaking. Margaux takes hold of my hand.

The ceremony is swift but touching. They can't take their eyes off each other, both full of love as they say "I do." They found each other, amidst this whole crowd.

As we leave the town hall, after all the rose petals and bubbles, after all the hugs and kisses and congratulations, I throw myself into the arms of my big sister, who, officially, is no longer a Delorme.

I urinate into the glass and dip the stick in it.
I place the test on the roll of toilet paper.
I stop myself from looking for five minutes.

We've been trying for six months, I'm sure this is the one.
I made sure I always raised my legs after we had sex.
Apparently, the missionary position is the ideal one.
Margaux got pregnant after a month.
We must put together a list of names.
I heard that some parents called their baby Boghosse—to sound like "beau gosse," a dish?
Or the legend of the family who called their daughter Clitorine.
I hope her father will manage to find her.
ONE MINUTE
I feel really good about this.
I read that you should seek advice after a year.
I hope we won't reach that stage.
What if I had a quick look?
No, I'll be disappointed.
If it's a girl, we'll go for Agathe as the middle name.
TWO MINUTES
I've never had such sore breasts.
Has to be a good sign.
It feels so long, having to wait a month each time.
Last month, I really believed that was it.
I wonder who I'll tell first.
Maybe Agathe.

Maybe Mima.
I'll tell Alex when he gets home this evening.
THREE MINUTES
I bought some bootees, for the announcement.
He's going to be so happy.
We'll have to move, the apartment will get too small.
Hope I don't get morning sickness.
Margaux vomited right up to the birth.
It would be good if our kids weren't too far apart in age.
FOUR MINUTES
Nearly there.
I must get a new watch, this one's too slow.
Sacha.
That's nice, Sacha.
As good for a girl as for a boy.
I so can't wait to be a mother.
I hope I'll do better than mine did.
My breasts really are very sore now.
I think I feel nauseous.
Three.
Two.
One.
FIVE MINUTES

I take a deep breath, grab the stick, and look at the result window. One line. I check in the instructions, I've already read them, and yet I hope that, this time, they'll tell me the opposite.

There's the verdict in capital letters, without appeal.

I throw the test and my disappointment into the trash can, wash my hands, press the pedal of the trash can again, it opens, I check one last time and then put the bootees away.

8:00 P.M.

Walking past the cinema, we saw they were showing *Titanic* in 3D. To mark the 25th anniversary of the movie, it was back on the big screen. We clearly couldn't let such an occasion pass us by.

The cinema was almost empty. So, it's possible for people to know that Jack and Rose are nearby and to resist them. Fascinating! Personally, if I happen to come across the movie on TV, whatever the time, whatever my schedule, I have to watch it right to the end.

"At least this time, you can't spoil it for me," Agathe says, putting on her 3D glasses.

"I'm going to keep hearing about that until the day I die."

"Of course. How can you expect me to forget something so traumatic?"

The movie begins. From the first few seconds, the music gets to me. Out of the corner of my eye, I see Agathe watching me.

"I made a bet that you'd blub within ten minutes," she whispers. "But you've smashed the record!"

I don't know why this movie has such an effect on me. The first time I watched it, I was seventeen, and nothing had ever moved me so much. I was going out with Loïc, and I remember considering leaving him because, suddenly, my own love story seemed pretty dull compared with that of Rose and Jack. And then there were all those lives snatched away, that tragedy unfolding as if you were right there. Strangely, although I had lost my father, it was this movie that taught me that everything could dramatically and suddenly change. For the developing young woman I then was, *Titanic* wasn't merely a movie, it was a command to savor the small joys, to write the script of my own life, to make the most of it. Through constant repetition, such notions are trivialized and become banal, if not corny, then at least naïve. And yet, when I think about it, nothing seems more important to me. To enjoy the journey. Reach the destination with no regrets. Realize that all that exists is the here and now, recognize the small joys, and not burden yourself with all the rest.

I'm convinced that this movie influenced my trajectory. That's the power of works of art, they can change a life.

8:43 P.M.

A few seats away from us, a guy is munching noisily. Poor fellow, he doesn't know what he's risking. Agathe can't stand mouth sounds, so, if you inflict them on her during *Titanic*, she's capable of the worst.

8:47 P.M.

She leans towards him:

"Excuse me, monsieur. Are you eating nails?"

I shrink into my seat.

9:22 P.M.

Rose and Jack are on the prow, the sun is setting. It's their first kiss. Tears prick my eyes.

"Emma?"

"What?"

"Jack and Rose are on a boat. Jack falls into the water, what's left?"

"Stop it, Agathe."

9:28 P.M.

"D'you know why the movie lasts three hours and fourteen minutes?" Agathe asks.

I shake my head.

"Because that's the precise length of time it took the liner to sink. See, I know more than you on the subject!"

"Stop talking, it's the drawing scene."

Nothing must interrupt the drawing scene. It's when the tension makes my starry-eyed girl's heart race, when a stick of charcoal becomes erotic. When the movie first came out, all my schoolmates took up drawing, clearly believing that would be enough to give them Jack Dawson's charm.

9:38 P.M.

I've seen this movie about twenty times, and yet, for a reason that's beyond me, each time the iceberg appears and the crew try to avoid it, I hope they'll succeed.

Agathe's hand grips the armrest.

10:17 P.M.

My favorite scene.

Rose jumps out of her lifeboat to get back to the liner and back to Jack. "You jump, I jump, right?"

I lay my hand on Agathe's.

11:02 P.M.

Back to the one hundred-and-one year-old Rose.

"Now you know there was a man named Jack Dawson and that he saved me in every way a person can be saved. I don't even have a picture of him. He exists now only in my memory."

I let out a gulp. Those words finish me off.

11:07 P.M.

The lights come up, Céline Dion sings, I don't dare look at

Agathe. I've been crying non-stop for fifty minutes, I'm going to hear about it for the rest of the evening.

I stand and pick up my bag, she doesn't move. I wait a few seconds, but she remains seated.

"Agathe?"

She looks up at me, and I see. Her face is flooded in tears, her eyes are red, her nose is running, her chin quivering, and her mouth downturned. She tries to look normal, to smile at me, perhaps thinking I won't notice a thing, but I get a massive fit of the giggles. She gazes at me, puzzled, almost offended, so I tell her it's the two of us making me laugh, the sisters who want everyone to know that they're tough, but are reduced to puddles as soon as someone dies at the end.

"Well, no, I'm totally fine," she tells me. "Honestly, it had no effect on me."

11:35 P.M.

I leave the cinema in the same state as the first time. Wanting to gorge on life. These past few years, I let life decide for me, I became wrapped up in the day to day, while time slipped through my fingers, and I lost sight of the seventeen-year-old Emma. I forgot her determination to make the most of every moment.

The scooter sets off, I close my eyes, wrap my arms around my sister, and let the warm breeze caress my face.

I've invited eleven people. Mima has prepared enough food to last us three weeks, Lucas has brought some chairs to seat everyone, Emma, Alex and my colleagues from the home came with bottles, my friend Julie made mini pavlovas, and my friend Amélie stopped off to buy bread and cheese. All the people that matter are here for my housewarming party. I don't yet know if Diego counts, but I suggested he come, and he immediately accepted. We've been seeing each other for a month. I really like him, but I'm trying not to get carried away (I've just chosen my wedding dress and the names of our children).

"You've got a splendid view," Mima says to me, quietly.

"I need at least that to replace you."

I have to stand on the washing machine to see it, but the sea is definitely there. I brought in the final box yesterday, and tonight I'll spend my first night here. I took my time. Even if I'm only moving two kilometers away, leaving Mima breaks my heart.

Ever since I signed the rental lease, I've been trying to convince myself that it's good news. Mom keeps saying that, at my age, it's time I live on my own, and she's right. And yet this evening, while the music and laughter celebrate this new life, there's a painful lump in my throat.

"Come and have a bite to eat," Mima says, as if she'd sensed it. "I made goat-cheese pastries, you love them."

I quit ruminating to go back to my guests. We gather around the low table, some on the sofa, others on the chairs, and some even on the carpet. Everyone gets acquainted—my sister's talking to Linda, my fellow care worker, Alex is laughing with Diego and Lucas, Mima is enjoying seeing Julie and Amélie again. Mixing different worlds is always tricky, but occasionally, glorious universes are the result.

We even dance, at one stage. Lucas rifles through my CDs and plays music that I'd never have admitted listening to, but we can't help bopping to.

The party goes on, the joy of the others seeps into me, I become porous to happiness. My sadness finally evaporates.

Mima is starting to feel tired, we clear the table to serve the dessert. Julie puts the pavlovas on side plates and hands them around to the guests.

"This is delicious!" Mima raves. "The meringue is perfect, not easy to achieve."

"It works really well with kiwis and clementines," Emma agrees.

"Will you slip me the recipe?" Linda asks.

"I've never eaten anything so good," Diego adds.

Julie's on cloud nine. She thanks everyone, and Diego lays it on even thicker:

"Admit it, you stopped off at the bakery before coming here."

She laughs:

"I swear I didn't, I spent hours making them."

"Well, they sure weren't wasted. If there's one left, it's mine!"

"I'm not hungry anymore," Lucas says. "Want to finish mine?"

My guy grabs the plate and wolfs down the dessert. I can feel the lump in my throat returning and worsening. He's being absurd, heaping praise on her like she's discovered a life-saving vaccine. What's gotten into all of them? Is this my party, or Julie's?

"Agathe, you've just got to learn how to make that!" he says, putting his spoon down.

"You have two hands, I believe."

Judging by the sudden silence, my infuriation has been registered. I can feel my blood boiling in my veins. I'm a volcano on the verge of erupting.

"Why are you speaking like that?" he asks.

"Firstly, because I'm not your cook. If you fancy eating something, *make it yourself. It's not only women who cook, welcome to the 21st century, my boy."*

"But I never said that!"

"I'm not done, let me speak! Secondly, because if you love Julie's desserts so much, just ask her to make you some."

"You think I'm flirting with her? Are you kidding?"

"Well, it was hardly subtle."

"I really didn't get that impression," a distraught Julie chips in.

Mima stands up and comes to rest her hand on my shoulder.

"Come now, my darling, we're here to have fun. Would you like some tiramisu? I popped it in the fridge, I'll go fetch it."

"I'm out of here," Diego declares, heading for the door. "You're off your head!"

"No need for insults as you go," my sister snaps at him.

"Come on, we can sort this out!" Lucas exclaims. "I'm sure Diego only meant to be polite."

"You can sort it out," Amélie whispers in my ear. "You did hit quite hard."

"Everyone out."

All eyes are on me.

"EVERYONE OUT, I SAID!"

"Agathe," Mima sighs.

"You're all ganging up on me, like he's in the right. So just leave with him."

"Gagathe," Emma tries.

"I don't want to see any of you anymore! The party's over!"

I storm off and lock myself in the bathroom. After a few minutes I hear the front door close. Anger is consuming me, I don't know what to do with it. I scream to let out my rage. I insult myself, I kick the wall. I bite my hand as hard as I can, tooth marks are left on my thumb. I hate them. I hate myself. I want to die.

That's it, I'm thirty. Strange to think I'm the age my father never was. I was long convinced that I'd die at twenty-nine, like him. Until yesterday, I saw signs everywhere, but I've made it. I'm older than he'll ever be.

As I reach the same ages as them, I realize how young my parents were. They were eighteen when I was born. Mom often told me that it was an accident, but they'd immediately decided to keep me.

At my age, she had two children of twelve and seven. I always saw my parents as old folks, and now I'm their age. Did they, like me, wonder how you can have an adult body yet still feel adolescent? Often, I feel overwhelmed by responsibilities, I become conscious of my age, but my childhood seems so recent. Did they feel that, too? Will I still feel that when I'm a mother?

If I ever am.

As a birthday present, I've just received the email I've been waiting for since the embryo transfer. The IVF didn't work. Second try, second failure. Alex tells me we'll get there. I'd like to be as sure as him. Sometimes I feel like giving up.

After a year of trying without success, we sought medical advice. We went through a battery of tests, and the blame fell on me. I suffer from endometriosis, I have lesions on my Fallopian tubes. Which also explains the horrendous pain during my periods, which nothing eased, and which my mother accused me of faking. She'd call me "a fussbudget," when I felt as if my innards were being ripped apart.

The gynecologist was honest: the chances of having a baby aren't great. I can't bear the injections, blood tests, treatments, hormones, false hopes, waiting, not anymore. I can't bear not knowing anymore if I'll be a mother one day. Everyone tells me that by overthinking it, I'm creating a block. Margaux advises me to go on vacation, she says a friend of hers succeeded in getting pregnant by letting go. Even Alex sometimes reproaches me for turning it into an obsession.

I feel alone, facing this void. I'm becoming bitter, envious of my friends whose bellies fill out. I don't understand why we don't have the right to that happiness, when it's so easy for others.

Agathe tells me it's normal, that such feelings will pass once I hold my baby in my arms. Even that annoys me. How can she be sure it'll happen, and how does she know what I will feel?

I'm going to end up sour and alone.

My phone vibrates. It's a message from my sister, wishing me happy birthday for the seventh time today. She must be aiming for thirty messages.

I switch off my phone and go back to bed.

12:23 A.M.

We picked up doner kebabs and fries on the way home. We settle on the swing seat. The stars are doing their thing, and it's still warm, despite the hour. We can hear cats fighting, in the distance.

"I hope it's not Robert Redford," Emma says.

"Maybe he's fighting with his brother. It can happen, doesn't mean they don't love each other."

Emma stares at me, no doubt wondering how so much subtlety can reside in a single person.

"Sometimes, they can find no other solution," she replies.

Silence descends, the tension mounts, I sense that now's the time, that we're finally going to have the discussion I'm waiting for. She eats one fry, then another, and dives in:

"I didn't want to abandon you. I've spent my life putting others before me. You, in particular. I stifled my desires, my needs, for yours. I didn't have to force myself, it came naturally, and it gave me pleasure. I tried to support you through your anxieties, to be there whenever you needed it. I tried to keep up with you, on your roller-coaster rides, but at a certain point, I don't know, I just couldn't understand you anymore. I got the feeling you were making no effort at all. Anger built up inside me. I had to escape, had to cut myself off. When Alex was offered a post in Alsace, I didn't think twice. I could have moved and continued to see you, but I needed a real break. A life without any surprises, a stable, calm life. I thought it would last a few weeks, a few months at most, but five years went by in a flash. I heard your news, I spoke regularly with Mima, and that was enough for me.

I didn't want to be involved anymore. Just a back-row spectator. I'm really sorry I didn't explain this to you, I think I was scared that, if I spoke to you, I'd give in. I didn't want to abandon you, I just wanted to save myself."

She lets a moment go by, then asks if I'm angry with her.

"At one time, I was angry with you, yes. At first, I was worried, when Mima told me you'd left to live in Alsace. You usually told me everything, and then, on something so important, total silence. I couldn't understand. Then I felt abandoned and was angry with you. Beyond angry. I was furious with you like I've never been furious with anyone. I needed time to understand. You know, even I would have left me, if I could have."

She lays her hand on my thigh. I continue:

"Truly, Emma, I understand you. Bipolar disorder is hard for the person who suffers from it, but also for those around them. I wouldn't swap you for anyone, for no other sister, you were perfect."

"You think so?"

"You're fishing for compliments! I think so even more than I'm telling you. Without you, I don't know how I'd have got through childhood. Oh no, you're not going to start blubbing again!"

She wipes her nose on her sleeve:

"You, too, you're the best sister in the universe."

"Right, enough of that, let's talk about serious things. You're not finishing your doner?"

She stares wide-eyed at me and takes a big bite of her filled pitta:

"Dream on. You're a great sister, but don't push your luck."

2:14 A.M.

I hadn't had an anxiety attack for ages. It isn't massive, but unpleasant enough for Morpheus to deny me his embrace. Spinning around in my head are Emma's words, my own, those five squandered years, desires for tomorrow. I've been tossing and turning for more than an hour, I try "heart coherence", focus all my attention on my breathing, but nothing stops the racket in my head. I know of only one thing capable of soothing me.

I get out of bed and go to the room Emma's sleeping in. The shutters are open, like every night, the moon lights my way. I slide into her little bed, she jumps, I reassure her, she grumbles, moves over to make room, slips her arm around me, and I fall asleep.

H ello?"

"Gagathe, I'm pregnant!"

"What? No, really?"

"Yes, oh my god, I can't believe it, at last! I'M PREGNANT! I thought I'd never say those words!"

"Oh, Emma, I'm so happy for you! I knew it would happen, it had to!"

"You're the first person I'm telling. I don't want to give Alex the news by phone."

"Are you calling me from the bathroom?"

"No, I've just received the results from the lab by email. But if you insist, I can go to the bathroom."

" . . . "

"Agathe?"

"What?"

"Are you crying?"

"Not at all, you are!"

"Ha ha ha! I can hear it, you liar!"

"I'm going to be an auntie."

"You're going to be a super auntie."

"I promise you I am. I'll buy my niece or nephew noisy toys, teach them swearwords, take them clubbing, make them listen to good music and watch good movies, but having said that, don't count on me for the dirty diapers."

"I keep rereading the email, to be sure I'm not dreaming. I mustn't get carried away. I could still have a miscarriage."

"Do get carried away, please. Lap up this happiness. All will go well, and in nine months, you'll be a mommy."

" . . . "
"Are you crying?"
"No, you are."

M iss?"
It's taking up all the space, this minuscule life in my belly. I stroke it, speak to it, give it pet names. I imagine what's going on in there, I bought two books that inform me, day by day, of the size and developments of my baby. It's the size of a strawberry and all its organs are in place. The gynecologist did an ultrasound in his office, we couldn't see much, but we heard its heartbeat. Alex cried.

"Miss?"

The first official ultrasound is in two weeks' time. I thought I was calm, but then made the mistake of looking at some medical chatrooms and learned lots of things I'd have preferred not to know. I already love this baby so much. I didn't know you could worry like this about a person you don't know.

"Hey, Miss!"

I'm not feeling too sick, occasional nausea, but nothing I can't get over. There are certain smells I can't bear anymore, like those of flowers and coffee. Which I've quit drinking, I'm on the herbal tea. I'm eating vegetables, too. It took sharing my body for me to start taking care of it.

"Miss, are you doing this on purpose?"

I study myself in the mirror every morning and am convinced my belly has got bigger. Alex says it hasn't, but I can see it. I can't wait for everyone to see it. I can't wait to feel it moving. I can't wait to hold it in my arms. I can't wait to—"

"Miss! Are you with us?"

A hand is shaking my shoulder.

"Mathis? What are you doing there?".
"We've been calling you for an hour now, your head's in the clouds! We've all finished the exercise, can we correct it now?"
It's taking up all the space, this minuscule life in my belly.

8:09 A.M.

On our last morning before leaving, Agathe insisted on coming swimming with me. I didn't sleep all night. I could feel her lying so peacefully against me, I was scared to wake her. It's time, I have to talk to her.

We tear our clothes off and run to the water.

"Wet your nape!" I shout to Agathe.

"Okay, Mima!"

She splashes me as she goes past, I push her, she falls headfirst, grabs a handful of sand and throws it at my stomach. The pain makes me double up.

"Stop faking!"

She sees I'm not kidding.

"Are you OK?"

"I had stomachache last night, must be the doner kebab."

"Want us to go back?"

"Dream on! Last to reach the arched rock gives the other one a massage."

We jump the waves, we dive, we swim, Agathe pulls ahead after only a few meters, but I fight to the end. I get there long after her, out of breath.

"Who'd have thought I'd be fitter than you one day?" she crows.

"Not me! You had all the endurance of a flat tire, I'm impressed."

I let myself float on my back. The sea's a little choppy, it rocks me. I make the most of this sensation, of this last time, tomorrow morning I won't be able to come and swim. My train leaves late morning, and I must first return the car to the rental agency.

Drops bounce on my face. I open my eyes, a gray cloud covers the blue. I think of our dance in the rain, the other evening, and decide not to flee the downpour. I let the water stream over my forehead, lips, eyelids, carry my body, I spread out my arms, my legs, relax my limbs. I'm at one with the water. Agathe's fingers flutter on mine then hold them, I turn my head, she's floating like a log, serenely, beside me. I imagine us seen from the sky, floating in the vastness, alone and together, and I feel enormously lucky to have her.

We remain there for hours, doubtless less, maybe more. The rain has stopped when we come out. The seagull man is there.

"Morning, Léon!" Agathe calls to him.

He stares at her, frowning, but doesn't reply.

"I'm almost disappointed," I say. "I'd have liked a final friendly word before I leave."

"He doesn't dare, with me. With the staff at the care home, he's unpleasant, but not insulting. With the other residents, however, there's no stopping him. Last week, he told Madame Rainault to eat her dead. She still hasn't gotten over it.

I can't help but laugh, imagining the scene. We sit on our towels facing the sun, which is reaching its zenith.

"We mustn't linger too long, I have a surprise for you," Agathe announces.

"Oh shit."

"Well, thanks a lot."

"I'm wary of your surprises. Remember that time you took me to the skating rink. My dignity must still be sprawled there, on the ice."

She bursts out laughing.

For one last time, I admire the ballet of the seagulls around the man with white hair, then Agathe declares it's time to go.

"Have a nice day, Léon!" she says, drawing level with him.

He doesn't even glance at her.

"All the best, monsieur!" I, in turn, call out.

And then, to my great delight, he's polite enough to reply to me: "Get lost, you shit shovel!"

We caught the first train. Charged across the station. Stopped a few times for Mima to catch her breath. Jumped into a taxi. Ignored the traffic lights.

We were allowed to wait in a small room.

We heard moaning, thought we recognized her voice.

Alex went out for some air: "It'll be a while yet, the doctor said."

Only one person could go and see her. I was dying to, but I let Mima go instead.

We ate a disgusting sandwich and read a celebrity magazine, bought from the store at reception.

We learned that Lorie was quitting singing and that Mickaël Vendetta even existed.

We heard a baby crying. Felt our hearts race. Waited. Realized it wasn't ours.

Mima dozed off, head against the wall, mouth open.

I counted her snores.

We saw two women go into the room.

We saw that they didn't come out.

We heard sounds of encouragement, groans.

We held hands.

We heard a tiny, mewing cry.

Alex came out, pushing a small, transparent cot in front of him.

We saw his little nose, his minuscule hands, his long lashes.

We met Sacha.

I should be happy.

For years I've lived for this. I subjected myself to treatments, tests, disappointments, thought we'd never make it, never be parents.

I had a wonderful pregnancy, tainted only by the fear of losing him. I loved him the second I knew he'd settled inside me. At each new ultrasound, my heart swelled a little more with love.

I counted the days until his birth, kept impatience at bay by decorating his room.

I imagined I'd feel serene, totally fulfilled, with my baby in my arms.

I should be happy. And yet I feel like dying.

I'm exhausted.

My breasts are sore.

I'm crying all the time.

I worry when he spits up, when he doesn't spit up, when his poo's hard, when he doesn't poo, when he cries, when he doesn't cry, when he sleeps a lot, when he doesn't sleep.

I search everywhere for the serenity I'd conjured up in my mind.

I'm nothing but a mass of anxiety and despair.

I hear him crying.

Alex has returned to work.

Agathe pops her head around the door:

"Take it easy, I'll see to him."

I didn't want to tell her I was in a bad way, but Alex didn't know how to help me anymore. She cut short her vacation in Spain to come to me.

Even with her, I can't manage to pretend.

For the first time it's not me taking care of her.

The day after she got here, she dragged me off to the doctor. He spoke of postnatal depression, prescribed some medication.

I came away staggered.

I shouldn't be depressed.

I've just had a baby, I should be happy.

9:34 A.M.

"First dibs!" Agathe cries as we arrive back at Mima's.

She charges up the stairs to take a shower. It's usually me that wins, but for the last day, I can give her the victory.

While waiting for my turn, and to find out what surprise she's got for me, I settle in the armchair. Sunlight bursts through the window and spills over my thighs. Only the tick-tock of the clock disturbs the silence. That sound terrified my sister when she was little. Papi would muffle it with fabric and foam.

Agathe's phone rings. A second time. A third time. I get up to catch it, it might be urgent. On the screen, "MOM" in capital letters. I don't allow myself time to think, I answer it.

"Hi Mom."

"Hi Agathe, you don't sound good, your voice is odd."

"It's Emma."

"What's she gone and done now?"

"No, it's Emma speaking to you. Not Agathe."

A brief silence.

"Oh, sweetie! It's been so long! How are you? Agathe told me you were together, and I'll admit I wanted to come, but she threatened never to speak to me again if I did. I've already lost one daughter, don't want to lose a second!"

She laughs loudly. Her awkwardness is catching.

"I'm well. And you?"

"Oh, me, it comes and goes. Can't complain. Two more years till I retire, and I'm starting to get osteoarthritis. But your sister must have told you that . . . Well, no, silly of me, I'm sure you don't talk about me."

"Shall I tell Agathe to call you back? She's having a shower."

"Yes, please. You're leaving tomorrow, right?"

"Yes."

"Can I really not come and see you? I'm four hours away, I can be there this evening."

"No, Mom, I'm really sorry. I'd rather not."

"Why did you answer the phone, if you don't want to speak to me?"

"Because I want to tell you something."

"Oh?"

I don't feel like it anymore. I regret answering, should have stuck with my initial decision never to speak to her again. But I'm here now, so I'll get on with it.

"You hurt me, Mom. You finished us off."

"Right, I'll . . . "

"Please listen to me. I have a mark from your belt buckle on my thigh, it will never go away. But it's inside that I'm most scarred. I have no confidence in myself, I never think I'm as good as others, making a phone call is an ordeal, I'm wary even of the people I love the most, *especially* of those I love the most. I get insomnia, can't handle anyone coming up behind me, don't like being surprised, saying 'I love you' is an effort, I can't sleep in the dark, I'm convinced I'm a bad mother, I can't bear the smell of patchouli anymore, I jump when a door slams, I hate my reflection, because it resembles yours."

At the other end, I can hear her shortness of breath.

Agathe comes into the sitting room, her hair wet. She understands immediately and takes my hand in hers. I put the phone on speaker, so she can hear.

"Is this some kind of revenge?" Mom whispers.

"Please, Mom, I'm nearly done. I'm not telling you to do harm to you, but to do good to myself."

"I don't have to listen to all this spiteful stuff! You want to make me suffer? I know very well that I hurt you. That I hurt both of you. It's easy to rewrite history, to point to me as the nasty one, but it was never that simple, sweetie. There was this great emptiness inside me. I tried to get better. You saw how I tried. Emma, you did see, didn't you? You also reproached me for leaving, to get treatment, but I had no choice. And anyhow, you weren't that easy yourself. I felt the judgment in your eyes, even if you said nothing. Life outside isn't rosy, I wanted you to understand that, your sister, too, I wanted to help you, teach you to toughen up. And look how you turned out, hey? You see, I didn't get everything wrong."

Agathe squeezes my hand.

"Right, Mom, I just wanted to tell you that I forgive you. I'm not angry anymore. I even manage to find excuses for you."

She doesn't respond.

"Mom?"

I look at the screen, she's hung up.

Agathe hugs me:

"Well done. I'm proud of you. I just can't do it myself. Perhaps because I have fewer memories, thanks to you. I know she'll never change, but I can't seem to draw a line under her." She stands up. "Remind me never to get on the wrong side of you. Fucking hell, girl, you use live ammunition!"

I've just realized that I haven't stuck my nose out the door for a week now. Since I quit my job, I'm not obliged to go out anymore, so I stay indoors, in the cool. Mima tried to make me change my mind, convinced that I was making a stupid mistake, that the job was made for me. Which is what I thought, too, at first. But my enthusiasm just evaporated. I'd been going reluctantly, sometimes not even waking up in the morning. I'll find something else.

I ought to wash myself, though. The other day, David commented that I hadn't used the shower, so I turn it on a little every day, pour some gel into the tray, and lightly dampen the towel. My hair's dirty, but I feel tired just thinking about washing it, untangling it, leaving the conditioner in, rinsing it.

He's starting to annoy me, anyhow. I was happy for him to move in with me, but if it's to keep me under surveillance, it's not going to work. The other day he came home at midday, wanted to eat with me. Bad luck: I was sleeping. He was pissed off, shocked that I could get up so late. If that's life as a couple, I prefer my vibrator.

Lucas insists I come surfing; I don't feel like it. Mima insists I come to eat; I don't feel like it. I just want to be left in peace. I close the shutters and, between naps, I watch TV. Anything, so long as it's not about war, insecurity, unemployment, poverty, pollution, politics, harassment, embezzlement, illnesses, deaths, accidents, violence. Everything depresses me, everything scares me, I can't see colors anymore.

What's the point of all this?

Life's so futile.

Emma bombards me with messages, I can't be bothered to reply. Doing the slightest thing demands too much effort.

My hours are empty, same as my existence. I just want to sleep. Take a sleeping pill. And just sleep.

Y ou wouldn't like to go and live in the Basque Country,
would you?"
Alex stares, wide-eyed:
"You'd like to go there?"
"I really would, yes."
"Because you can see yourself living there, or for your sister?"
"She's not doing well. For several months now, she's been going
under, I feel powerless here."
"I understand, but our jobs are here, the little one's crèche, our
friends. And anyhow, we're barely two hours from Anglet!"
"Two hours, that's pretty long to go and see her every day."
He sighs.
"I understand, sweetie, I really do. And you know I adore your
sister. But you can't always save her. At some stage, she's going to
have to take charge of herself. She'll soon be thirty, she's not a kid
anymore."
"I know . . . "
"We can't come running as soon as she's struggling. You go there
almost every weekend as it is, which is already a lot, isn't it?"
"Yes, of course. But she's my little sister, I'm worried for her.
I've always felt that this world was too tough, that she didn't have
big enough shoulders. When I think of her, I see her as tiny, surrounded by towering mountains."
"Maybe she needs to prove to herself that she can cope. You
know, overprotecting her isn't helping her."
"That's one of the dumbest things I've ever heard."
He laughs.

"That's true, I realized it as I was saying it. But you can't live for her. You're there, she knows that. She's not alone. And there's also your grandmother, your uncle, your aunt . . . "

"What a joke! When Uncle Jean-Yves discovered that Mima had helped Agathe with paying her rent last month, he went ballistic. He threatened Mima that he'd place her under supervision, and sent a message to Agathe accusing her of being an idler. Great support he is."

"Fine, we'll forget about your uncle and aunt then. Go and spend some time over there during the next vacation if you like. Or suggest she comes here. But we can't just chuck up everything to go and live near her. D'you understand that?"

I nod my head. I know he's right.

I switch my computer back on and resume my search for an apartment in Anglet.

1:23 P.M.

Emma parks near the harbor. I thought we'd never make it on time, never known anyone who drives so slowly. I'd have gotten here faster moonwalking. She still doesn't know what we're doing here, despite all her questions throughout the journey, but the surprise will soon be revealed.

"Are we going sailing?" Emma asks, as we walk along a pontoon.

"How perceptive!"

She claps her hands in delight. When she discovers the purpose of this boat trip, she may well be doing cartwheels.

Julie and Amélie are waiting for us on the boat. Emma has met them several times but doesn't know what they do. They quickly explain it to her.

They are both biologists. Part of their work involves studying the cetaceans that live in the Gouf de Capbreton.

"It's an underwater canyon that's more than 4,000 meters deep," Julie explains to my sister. "What makes it exceptional is that it starts just a few hundred meters from the coast."

"Its biodiversity level is high, particularly its many species of cetacean," Amélie continues. "Our role is to study them to understand them better and raise people's awareness to protect them. Agathe told us you were passionate about dolphins?"

Emma's eyes are sparkling:

"Oh yes! I had a poster for *The Big Blue* on the wall in my room for ages, and I dreamt of seeing dolphins, swimming with them. I even wrote to the *Journal de Mickey* to ask them what studies I should do to work with dolphins, but I never got a reply."

The disappointment has clearly endured over the years, Emma frowns just remembering that let-down.

"I always knew Mickey Mouse wasn't to be trusted," I say.

"We're not going to swim with them, because we don't want to disturb them, but we'll try to spot some," Julie declares.

"For real?" Emma asks, looking at me.

"No, it was a joke, we're going to walk on water like Jesus. Are you ready?"

She laughs:

"I'm so happy, Gagathe! Let's hope we see lots of them!"

2:07 P.M.

She's not happy at all anymore. Well, that's the impression she's giving, unless throwing up over the rail makes her very happy.

The boat stops. Julie puts some headphones on and lets a cable sink into the water, at the end of which a microphone and a sort of dish antenna are attached.

"She's trying to locate them," Amélie explains. "In the middle of summer, it's trickier, there's lots of noise pollution with all the leisure boats. But you can still hear them."

After a while, Julie shakes her head: "Let's go and look further on."

5:34 P.M.

We still haven't seen any dolphins, but the good news is that Emma has quit feeding the fish. Julie has lowered the hydrophone at several locations, at various depths, without success.

Emma comes to sit beside me:

"I'm touched by your surprise."

"Oh, I just felt like seeing you throw up."

She rests her head on my shoulder.

"If you're that keen, I can throw up on you. It'll be my revenge for all those times you pooed in the bath."

"You're lying. Inventing memories for us."

She raises her head and gazes at the horizon. The blues of the sea and the sky merge together. Out of the corner of my eye, I see her wiping her cheek.

"I love you, Gagathe."

She turns towards me; in her eyes I see the same light as in that photo of twenty years ago, with Alex. She nudges me:

"Don't ask me to repeat that, you can't imagine how saying it pained me."

"Sorry, I thought I'd misheard! Fucking hell, let's celebrate, Emma's revealing her feelings!"

"If you want to make me regret doing so, you're doing a good job."

"So sorry, it gave me a shock."

She laughs.

"You're hard work, Gagathe. So, I'm not going to say it again!"

"That's okay, I heard it, and there are witnesses. Girls, did you hear it, too?"

Laughing, Julie and Amélie confirm that they did.

At that moment, a few meters from the boat, a fin cleaves the water, then two fins, then six.

Emma is mesmerized, the dolphins leap, frolic all around us.

"My god," she murmurs. "Are you seeing this magnificent show?"

I see it. But it's something else that moves me: my sister's child-like delight, and the look of wonderment in her eyes.

7:17 P.M.

Robert Redford is in front of the gate when we get back. He knows his way, he doesn't need us to find Georges's house. And yet I scoop the cat up and head for Mima's sweetheart's home.

Emma follows me without asking any questions, she has understood.

The discovery of that painting had knocked me sideways. I discovered that my grandmother could have had a sex life, that her children weren't delivered by a stork, it was a lot to take in. I didn't have the strength to say a thing to Georges; I handed him his painting, he thanked us, he left, end of story.

The door to no. 14 overlooks the street. I use the iron knocker. Georges opens, Robert Redford springs from my arms.

"Come in," he says, as though expecting us.

It's cool inside his house.

"I've just opened the shutters, I keep them closed all day," he explains.

We follow him along a corridor and emerge into a huge sitting room. Pieces of imposing furniture rest on a red-tiled floor. He indicates for us to sit on a brown leather sofa.

"Would you like something to drink?"

Emma asks for a glass of water, and I accept a glass of wine. While he's fetching them, my sister checks on my intentions.

"You know he's an elderly gentleman, Agathe."

"Why are you telling me that?"

"Be nice to him."

"Am I usually not nice?"

"You can be."

I don't get time to respond before Georges returns and sits opposite us:

"I imagine you have some questions."

The first one comes out of my mouth before my brain has time to tidy it up:

"Were you together? With Mima, I mean? Or do you have nude portraits of you with all your female neighbors?"

He laughs.

"It troubles me, betraying her secret, your grandmother was determined to keep it. But the loss is unbearable, and I have no one I can talk about her with."

"Why didn't she tell us?"

Emma throws me a dark look. I realize my tone was sharp, and try to make up for it:

"Why didn't she tell us, please?"

"Your grandfather had been dead for several years when we fell in love. But she knew how much you loved him, she feared hurting you. Time went by. On several occasions she announced that she was going to reveal everything to you, but in the end, she never found the right time."

He stares deep into space, seeming to gather his thoughts. We wait, silently, hanging on his memories of a Mima we didn't know. Finally, he continues:

"You know, she did resist. She battled with her feelings. She refused to love a man other than your grandfather. But love is stronger than the will. We were happy. Oh yes . . . supremely happy."

Georges's voice falters. There's a lump in my throat. Imagining Mima as a woman in love overwhelms me. I'm happy about this happiness I didn't know about.

"You never wanted to live together?" Emma asks.

"We thought about it several times, but our relationship was so perfect as it was, we feared spoiling it. We thought we had time. The years flew by so fast. And yet, we had a rule that we never broke: we'd see each other every day. Whether for hours or a few minutes."

"Impossible," I snap. "I lived with her for years, and even after that, came to see her often. I'd have known."

Georges looks at me as if I'd just realized that Father Christmas didn't exist.

"There wasn't a day when we didn't see each other," he insists, smiling.

My sister laughs:

"It's so like her, leaving us a surprise as an inheritance!"

8:14 P.M.
We leave Georges, promising to stay in touch.

"I like him," Emma declares, as we walk back to Mima's.

"I think I do, too."

"Not too hurt?"

"Of course not."

She knows me well enough to know I'm lying. Of course I'm hurt. I'd have wanted Mima to talk to me about Georges, to share her secrets with me as I shared mine with her. I'd have liked her not to lie to me, to spare herself that guilt. To spare me my guilt. The guilt I felt every time I left her. Imagining her alone in her house broke my heart. I felt like I was abandoning her. I would have been happy for her. What upsets me most is that she could have doubted that.

Going past the Garcias' house, I spot Joachim in the garden. He waves at me. I wave back, but with just one finger.

There's a knock on my apartment door. I don't know the
time. I haven't washed for three days and I smell of breaded
fish, but the person keeps knocking, so I open.

There are two of them. My uncle and my aunt. Going by their
expressions, they haven't come to play Monopoly.

"Mima told us you'd dropped eight kilos," he begins.

" . . . "

"Your grandmother doesn't need this. You must stop telling her
your problems, it upsets her, as you can imagine."

"You must pull yourself together," my aunt adds. "It's beyond
me, you have every reason to be happy."

"We can't stand for it anymore," he continues. "If you want to go
under, fine, but don't drag my mother down with you."

"I'm not dragging anyone down with me."

"You confide in her, you think that doesn't affect her?"

"It stinks in here," my aunt snaps, opening the window. "And
the sink's full of dirty dishes. You can't live in this state!"

The trial lasts about twenty minutes. The two prosecutors list
all the charges against me, while I listen in silence.

"You quit all your jobs."

"And you change partners as often as a shirt. Do you think your
father would be proud?"

"People are talking, you know. You're shaming the family. Do
you ever think of us?"

"We can't take it anymore, you've always been difficult, but it's
going from bad to worse."

"You must stop talking to Mima. You're going to end up killing her!"

"*You should go back home.*"

They kiss me and leave, no doubt satisfied that they've done their duty. I can imagine them congratulating each other for having shaken me up and having done so for my own good.

I sleep for twenty-four hours.

Mima calls me three times, I don't answer.

I can see no way out. I've been in this state for months now, and I can no longer envisage things getting better one day.

The only person I feel like talking to is Emma.

We talk for a long time. Mainly her. I don't even have the strength anymore.

"I'll be there tomorrow," she says. "You need some help. I'll take you to hospital, where you have to stay until you're better."

"No."

When she turns up the following day, I still say no, and yet I let her fill a bag with my things, drape a coat around my shoulders, lace my shoes, and take me to the psychiatric emergency department.

She'll probably never know it, but she saves my life.

We were up at the crack of dawn. We had breakfast in our room. It's a family room, we left the double bed to Mima, and I'm sharing the sofa-bed with Agathe.

Mima and I thought of the surprise to celebrate Agathe leaving hospital. "She needs to regain some weight," Mima declared. Italy was the obvious choice. Where better than the land of our roots to get her back on her feet?

Mima had been there twice as a child and once with Papi. We'd never been. When we were little, our grandmother would tell us that, if she won the lottery one day, she'd take us to discover the country of our ancestors. I can still see us, lying on her bed, asking her for a story to postpone bedtime, and her telling us about Romulus and Remus, the Palatine Hill, the flavors of ice cream, the scent of wisteria. But the story we loved best, and that made us shudder, was the one about the Bocca della Verità, the Mouth of Truth. She'd tell us how, as a child, she'd plunged her hand into the mouth of this marble mask, which, according to legend, was supposed to close on those who didn't tell the truth. She had indeed lied shortly before, to cover up some mischief of her little brother's. Her knees were knocking and heart racing as she awaited the verdict. My sister and I would be in that state, too, every time, even though we knew the happy ending.

Yesterday, when we arrived in Rome, it was the first thing we wanted to see. As we approached the mask, hands outstretched, I'm sure all three of us were ten years old again.

It's barely seven in the morning when we leave the hotel. It took some time to wake Agathe up. The antidepressants and tranquillizers she's been prescribed knock her out. She's rediscovered her taste for life but lost her enthusiasm. She's the sort who goes into raptures over a pebble, but she didn't react when we flew above the clouds. She told me she felt like she was inside a bubble, impervious to emotions. Shielded from her moods. If that's the price to pay so she doesn't suffer, I accept it, but I'm sad to see her so not herself.

We reach the Trevi Fountain. Mima is pleased, she wanted to get there before it's invaded by tourists. There are just a few people taking photos. A young bride and groom strike a pose.

Mima takes three coins from her purse and gives us one each.

"You have to throw it in and make a wish," she says.

"You know they collect a million euros every year?" Agathe says. "I don't know where it all goes, but it's a clever ploy!"

"It's far too early for cynicism," Mima retorts.

She asks a lady to take our photo, handing her the camera.

"At least you'll have one photo in focus," I say, as she slots in between us.

Agathe doesn't laugh, and yet it's one of our favorite jokes. Mima takes forever to take a photo, and the result is invariably blurred, which always greatly amuses us.

"Ready?" Mima asks, standing with her back to the fountain, as tradition dictates.

She's so happy to be here, with us. Even without having won the lottery.

"One, two, three!"

We each throw our coin backwards. I'm sure that Mima and I are silently making the same wish.

9:03 P.M.

"Could I come and visit you, over the next vacation?"

Emma nods:

"With pleasure. You'll see, our apartment isn't big, but it's in a good location."

"It's much too far from the sea to be in a good location."

"The children will be pleased to see you."

"I should hope so!"

For our last evening, we laid a rug out in the shade of the linden tree and threw together a picnic. Neither she nor I said so, but we didn't want to be with anyone else.

There's an end-of-vacation vibe. A joyful insouciance wrapped in nostalgia.

"I love you, too."

Emma smiles:

"You took four hours to reply, that's some delay."

"I missed you, big sister. You can't imagine how much."

She pours us both a glass of wine.

"I wasn't sure you'd agree to come," she says.

"You're kidding, it's all I was hoping for. And it was even better than I hoped. Hey! Why don't we have a week's vacation together every year?"

She doesn't reply but hands me a slice of bread with some feta on it. I'm already full (I've eaten so many cherry tomatoes, my innards are going to produce ketchup,) but I try it anyway.

"Are you happy?" she asks. "I mean generally. In your life."

The question surprises me, it's one I haven't asked myself in a long time. Which is, without any doubt, the best proof that I am happy.

I've spent most of my life feeling different, being swamped by my emotions, dependent on my moods, thinking, and almost accepting, that I'd never be able to find serenity. I wasn't aiming for happiness, firstly because I've never really understood what it was about, and then because it seemed more like an illusion than an objective. No one understood me, least of all me. I was the troublemaker, the girl you can't count on, whom you fear inviting, who goes too far, goes over the top, who wears you down, overwhelms you, exhausts you, the one you call less and less frequently, and end up leaving in a corner of the past. Most of my friends grew tired of those endless fresh starts. I get it. You support someone, help them back onto their feet, you're relieved, and then there's the collapse, again, the same words, the same old refrains, the feeling of not being heard, of not being useful. Mental illnesses cause collateral damage.

When I was depressed, I was there for no one, not even myself. It's quite something, depression. It's spoken about in a whisper, with eyes rolled, as if shameful, as if it's an act. The sick person is expected to pull themselves together, show some willpower, as if they enjoyed feeling like that, floundering in despair, as if they didn't hope to glimpse some light one day that would make the darkness bearable. I think depression scares people. They know that no one is immune to it. To see someone going under and realize your own powerlessness is frightening. I don't hold it against anyone, especially not my sister.

During my hypomanic phases, in that state of elation, I was buzzing with plans, I barely slept, I'd blow my salary in a single day, throw myself into new activities, fall in love, make love again and again, I was beautiful, intelligent, invincible. Everyone loved me, everyone wanted me around. I felt good. It never lasted, a few weeks at most. Sometimes I miss that euphoria.

Medication turned my ocean into a lake, my storm into a

summer morning. The side effects are difficult. At the start, I'd sometimes stop taking the drugs. As soon as they took effect, as soon as I was feeling better, I'd conclude that I wasn't ill, that I didn't really need them. Of course, a relapse awaited me, lurking behind the withdrawal symptoms. It would take Mima finding me in a bad way, and me seeing, in her eyes, the pain I was causing her, to understand that I had to continue with my treatment.

My sister, glass in hand, waits for my reply:

"I'm doing well. I'm doing really well."

She smiles.

"Those are the words I came to hear."

"And you?" I ask, lighting a cigarette.

"I'm happy, yes."

She seems, suddenly, to search within herself.

"I'm crazy about my kids, my husband's great, I'm passionate about my work, I grew up with Mima's love . . . and I have the most extraordinary sister on the planet."

"At the least!"

"To say the least, yes. If I could swap, I promise you I wouldn't want any other sister. Seriously, I've thought about it a lot lately, and I can say that I have a good life. The one I dreamt of."

"That's a worthy project, that. A good life. I'll put it right at the top of my list."

"Before or after the Jean Paul Gaultier show?"

I almost choke on my bread. My sister laughs at her bad joke and slips her arm around my shoulder.

"I hope you get your good life, my Gagathe."

11:59 P.M.

We exhausted every subject, pulled the memory thread—that time we dyed each other's hair and I ended up with green highlights; that day we left the hair-removing cream on for too long; that one when Mima caught us smoking behind the linden

tree—we ranked Mima's recipes in order of preference, did im-
pressions of Uncle Jean-Yves and Auntie Geneviève. I can't find
a comfortable position anymore, our bodies are telling us to go to
bed, Emma has a long drive, and yet we stay there, talking about
any old thing, simply to stretch time.

I arrive early at Mima's. It's our tradition—every Friday I come for lunch. I had training today and left work earlier than usual. I used the extra time to stop and buy bread and a dessert, hoping she hasn't made one. As I pull up on my scooter outside the gate, a man is leaving the garden. Mima is standing in front of the house.

"Hello, my darling! Oh, you shouldn't have, I've made pancakes!"

"Hi Mima. Who's he?"

"A neighbor looking for his dog. Come in, it's warm inside."

We eat in front of the TV news, that's her routine. She almost never watched the box when Papi was here. Now, it's become a companion.

"Any news of your sister?" she suddenly asks.

"Not for a few days. Last Monday, I think. Why?"

"She had her blood test yesterday, I believe."

"If she hasn't rung, it mustn't have worked."

Mima puts her fork down:

"Is there a problem between you two?"

"We fell out a bit."

"And that stops you from supporting her at this difficult time? She asks after you every time she calls me."

I roll my eyes.

"Mima, you know very well that I'm the nasty one. Emma is perfect, she does everything right, she's wonderful."

She laughs:

"Goodness me, what am I going to do with you two? I didn't

have a sister, just a little brother, and between us, too, there was sometimes a little jealousy. It's inevitable, you know."

"Well, number one, I'm not remotely jealous, and number two, I'd be amazed if Emma's jealous of me. She has no reason to be."

"And yet she recently told me that she'd have liked to be as funny and free as you. She even added that you were my little favorite."

"I don't believe you."

"You wouldn't dare call me a liar?"

"Apart from when you play Chinese checkers, you mean?"

"Cheeky!"

It's soon time for me to get back, Mima wraps two pancakes in some foil:

"For your afternoon snack."

"I've already eaten enough to last ten days!"

She winks at me:

"Seems you're my little favorite, so I have to spoil you."

"Did she really say that? That I was funny and free?"

"Really."

S acha is three years old. I can't get over it. And yet I'd swear
he was born just yesterday.

I wish I could preserve forever his lisp, his garbled words,
and his little arms around my neck. He says "in any case" in every sentence, asks me every morning if he can "woke up," follows
me everywhere with his mini vacuum cleaner when I'm doing the
housework, keeps saying "Mommy" all day long, and sometimes,
when I'm desperate to sleep, all night long, too. It took me some
time to enjoy this blessing. It took therapy and medication to haul
me out of the abyss. Now, my happiness can be so intense that it
hurts, makes me want to cry. Just by looking at my son.

"Come, Mommy!" he says, grabbing my hand and pulling me to
the fridge. "Godmother she want thocklit cake."

"Hey, you little rascal!" Agathe cries, laughing. "It's you who
wants cake, I didn't ask for a thing!"

He puts on his surprised face, but I'm not taken in. He's entirely
capable of passing the blame. The other day, when I asked him if
it was him who'd drawn on the wall with my lipstick, he shook his
head: "No way, in any case! It's teddy!"

Mima and Agathe have made the trip for the birthday party,
arriving yesterday. My mother, too, with Gérard, her new partner.
And Margaux, and Alex's brother are here. We're just waiting for
his parents now, and then Sacha can eat some thocklit cake.

"Come here, my little darling!" my mother says, lifting my son
into her arms.

He struggles, but she smothers his cheeks with noisy kisses,
while glancing at Mima:

"You love your granny, don't you Sacha? Say you love me!"

He manages to wriggle away and runs off to the bedrooms. Alex sets the drinks out on the table, I offer sweets to our guests. Agathe tells a story, everyone laughs. The jovial atmosphere helps me to forget this morning's test, for a while.

"We're a chair short," Agathe warns me.

"I'll go fetch the one in the bedroom."

I cross the corridor and pick up the chair that sits in a corner of our room. It's where Alex throws his clothes when he gets undressed, when he could put them straight into the wash, or away in a cupboard. Drives me crazy.

I think I hear a noise.

A sharp slap.

Crying.

I understand instantly. I run to Sacha's room, adjoining ours. My son is there, in tears, his little body racked with sobs, his arm gripped in my mother's hand.

7:56 A.M.

Emma tries to get up without waking me. Fails. Last night, for the first time ever, it was she who came to join me in my bed. She was shivering and shaking but didn't want to talk. She just slid up to me and clutched me like a teddy.

"I'm going to have my shower," she whispers. "Sleep a bit longer, if you like."

I close my eyes, but sleep has packed up and gone. All that's left is immense sadness. Saying goodbye to Mima's house and my sister on the same day is a lot.

8:10 A.M.

The aroma of coffee fills the kitchen.

"What time is your train?" I ask.

"11:24, I think. I must check."

"Is it direct?"

"No, I have to change in Paris."

The conversation seems like a way of avoiding saying we're sad. We're interrupted by the sound of the front door opening. Uncle Parking-ticket Machine and Auntie Wet Blanket greet us. I really must stop hanging out at home in my undies.

"You haven't left?" Jean-Yves asks, with surprise.

I look around us:

"Hold on, just checking. No, we haven't left."

"Weren't you supposed to leave yesterday?" Geneviève asks, clearly immune to any kind of humor. "We're not throwing you out, we've just come to fetch a few things."

"But since we're here, we'll have the keys back. You've not done any damage?"

He's not an uncle, he's a furuncle.

"I just broke the toilet," Emma replies. "We'd eaten spicy stuff, the bowl melted."

They don't react. Emma was the only one in their good books, today she's become as infra dig as me.

They help themselves to coffee, sit at the table, open the TV schedule and start doing a crossword. They clearly intend to stay here until our departure. I grab the chance to do something I've meant to do for a long time.

"Here, uncle," I go, handing him a coin.

"What's this?"

"I'm returning the twenty centimes that you lent me in August 1993 and have regularly asked me for ever since. I checked and, converting francs to euros and taking depreciation into consideration, I owe you exactly 4.8 centimes. But I've added on the interest and rounded up."

He takes the coin and thanks me. He was born missing a sense of irony.

I find Emma up in the bedroom, she's speaking out loud.

"What are you doing?"

"I'm thanking each room in the house, like the new owner advised us to."

Naturally, I scoff at her. But, discreetly, I, too, go around the house to thank it.

The bathroom for those "first dibs" battles with my sister, the lotions Mima would smooth over our hair, her lingering perfume, the bidet I'd secretly pee in when the toilet was occupied.

Dad's room for all those nights, all those dreams, those teenage sorrows, Mima scratching at the door to wake me.

Papi's and Mima's room for the trampoline-bed, the hiding-place cupboard, the drawer full of magical scarves, those nights when they'd both pretend not to notice me sneaking in between them.

The kitchen for the gnocchi, the zabaglione, Mima in her apron, the saucepan with leftover chocolate to lick, all those *Mamma mia!*s flying around (the kitchen was the only place Mima would speak Italian), the cupboards full of treats, the dish-soap bubbles.

The sitting room for those games of Chinese checkers Mima would cheat in, our TV nights under a throw, Mima's cuddles in the armchair, the sunlight dappling the floor, us chasing around the table armed with cushions, the cast-iron radiator I'd cling to in winter, Mima's voice, Papi's voice, Dad's voice, the voices of all my absent ones.

And then off we go.

9:12 A.M.

Emma tailed me to my place. I didn't have space on the scooter for all the belongings of Mima we'd kept.

"Have you lived here long?" she asks.

"Two years."

"It's bigger than the other place, you must be more comfortable."

"Yes, I feel good here. Right, I don't want to throw you out, but if you don't want to miss your train, you mustn't hang around."

"I know. But I . . . "

She goes quiet, just stands there for a moment, then hugs me. Tight. Very tight.

"This is homicide, Emma. You're suffocating me."

She lets go and looks at me:

"You promise you'll visit soon? The children will be happy to see you."

"Promise. Go on, off with you, before I blub again."

She hugs me one last time, plants a kiss on my cheek, and then off she goes.

J ulie and Amélie have legally registered their association. As of today, they're officially studying the cetaceans in the Gouf de Capbreton. To celebrate, we meet up at a nightclub. About a dozen of us, most of whom I already know, but not all.

It's the fourth night this week I've gone partying. This morning, I arrived late to work, got my knuckles rapped. Which really pissed me off. Strangely, when I leave work later than I'm supposed to (every evening), I don't hear a peep from them.

"To the cetaceans!" Julie cries, raising her glass.

"To the cetaceans!" we cry back, raising ours.

Anyhow, I don't give a damn. If they're not satisfied, they can fire me. I do a good job, the children adore me, so apart from being late a few times, they've got nothing to reproach me for. They don't deserve me. I can find other work whenever I like.

"Coming for a dance?"

It's one of Julie's friends, I don't know him. Not my type, but not repulsive, either.

We dance. I'm wearing my favorite black dress and my hair in a chignon. I've noticed a few looks, I feel sexy. I make for the bar, he doesn't take his eyes off me. He wants me.

He offers me a drink, we sit down. He puts his hand on my thigh, I let him. He talks into my ear, I don't catch everything, the music drowns his words, I lead him outside.

His car is parked in the street. We're quick about it. He doesn't even take his jeans off.

"I'm really sorry, I ripped your tights."

"Will you give me your number?"

"*I'd rather take yours. I'm married.*"

I return to the dancefloor with bare legs. The DJ plays Bruno Mars's "24K Magic," Julie and Amélie join me, and we dance into the wee hours.

Sacha's in hospital. I'm terrified.

I was teaching when his school phoned me. I only saw the message at recess. He'd already been taken to hospital. A colleague drives me there, I'm in no state to drive myself. The principal didn't see what happened, but she explained to me that Sacha fell off his chair during a painting class and had had convulsions afterward.

Alex is already there when I arrive. Tests are being carried out. He reassures me: Sacha is conscious, he'd been able to speak to him.

Those are the longest minutes of my life. On my phone, I look up the causes of convulsions, what I read makes me envisage the worst.

"I couldn't handle him dying."

"Why are you thinking like that? He's in good hands, there's no reason that would happen."

"Aren't you scared?"

"I'm concerned, of course, but I know everything will be fine."

I try to cling to his certainty, but anxiety has taken control. I want just one thing: to get my baby back and take him home.

My phone rings. It's Agathe. I don't answer. She calls again. I send her a text message:

"I'll call you back later."

"I've been dumped."

"I can't talk, I'll call you as soon as I can."

"Are you teaching?"

"No."

I don't tell her more so as not to worry her. She leaves it at that.

For the first time, I weigh up the sacrifices that protecting her demands of me.

I need her, but instead I'm thinking about her needs.

I don't leave any space for myself, and I don't give her the chance to support me. This pattern is starting to reach its limits. I sometimes begrudge her for receiving without giving, even though I don't allow her to give.

I put on the big-sister costume when Agathe was born, and I'm beginning to feel cramped in it.

After an unbearable wait, the doctor calls for us. Sacha is on a drip, lying under a sheet. He smiles when he sees me. I hold him in my arms, cover him with kisses, inhale his skin, feel his curls under my fingers, listen to his voice as if for the first time.

The encephalogram and MRI scan revealed nothing. From his teacher's description, Sacha had an epileptic fit. It could be an isolated incident and never happen again, just as it could be masking an illness. He must remain here, under observation, for two nights, after which, if all's well, he'll be able to come home.

Alex returns to the house to pack a bag, while a nurse transfers Sacha to a room. I follow them, I'm going to spend the night with him.

He soon falls asleep, thanks to my caresses and loving words.

I meet Alex at the hospital entrance to collect the bag. We fall into each other's arms, sobbing, out of both relief and anxiety.

Before going back up, I phone Agathe, determined to listen to my own needs, and allow myself to be comforted by my sister:

"Sacha's in hospital, he had an epileptic fit at school."

"Really? How's he doing?"

"They're keeping him in for observation, but they didn't find anything."

"Nerve-wracking. Keep me posted, okay?"

"Okay."

"You know, he dumped me by text message, that dickhead."

9:31 A.M.

I have to pull over onto the hard shoulder. I can't see the road, I'm crying so much.

I chickened out.

I didn't manage to do it.

I came to do it, and I'm leaving without having done it.

I let my tears wash away my distress, my fear, my feeling of guilt. After several minutes, they finally dry up. On the radio, Kyo are singing about their last dance.

I wipe my cheeks, and then make a U-turn.

I'm so sorry, I can't go on anymore. I love you all."

I leave the note in plain sight on the table.
I swallow the pills with some gin. One by one. The whole box.
I lie down in bed.

I send a text message to Emma.

I go back and forth every weekend to look after Agathe. She spent just a week in hospital, didn't want to stay any longer. We didn't tell Mima about it. She's too old to handle it.

I suggested to Agathe that she come and live with us, she refused. I was relieved. I felt guilty for being relieved.

She's doing better. She's back at work and is starting to go out again.

Sacha's calling for me. He often wets his bed.

I'm exhausted. I shout a lot.

I never finish my meals.

We've put the IVF treatment on hold. There's no way I could fall pregnant in this situation.

Alex supports me, but it's not enough. I'd like someone to carry me, breathe some strength into me. I can feel myself sinking.

"You still don't want to go and live in the Basque Country?" I ask Alex, right in the middle of supper.

"No, sweetie, not a good idea."

"Okay."

"Having said that, there's an interesting post that's just come up in Strasbourg."

He laughs, as if it were unthinkable. And yet, when he says "Strasbourg," what I hear is "leave."

"Apply."

He raises his eyebrows. He sees I'm not joking. He nods, and I help myself to more gratin.

10:48 A.M.

I'm lying on my bed getting depressed with my luminous firefly in my arms when there's a knock on the door. Emma doesn't wait for me to open, just walks right in. She sits on the bed beside me.

"I have to tell you something."

She's short of breath. I hold mine.

"They found something nasty inside me, cancer of the pancreas."

The blood drains out of me. I clasp my firefly, its head lights up.

"The chemo didn't work, or the radiotherapy."

Suddenly, it all makes sense. Her short hair. Her weight-loss. Her breathlessness. Her missing Mima's funeral.

"The tumor's in an awkward place." Her voice chokes. "They can't operate, my Gagathe."

I'm suffocating, my head's spinning. Everything's confused. I scream inside. I don't want to hear the rest.

She understands without my having to tell her. She nods and murmurs:

"I'm so sorry, little sister."

My body's shaking, I feel like vomiting. I stand up, my firefly falls to the floor, I hold Emma in my arms, as tight as I can. For the first time, I feel her letting go, leaning on me. I'm terrified. I squeeze her even tighter. I want to smother her pain. Crush her fear.

"I won't let you go, Emma. I promise you."

T he sky is a pale blue. The sun, just risen, casts a pink light over a cluster of clouds. The streets are almost deserted, I pass the odd car, and a few cats that bolt at the approach of my scooter.

It was still dark when I woke up. I clung to the hope of going back to sleep, tossed and turned for a while, but my thoughts surged and pushed me out of bed. My body and my brain have been totally at odds for months now, like a couple on the verge of divorce. While the former is lethargic, the latter throws open the windows, empties out all the cupboards, and scrubs the tiles with a toothbrush.

I got up from the sofa I've been sleeping on for a week, dressed myself in the dark, and left my apartment on tiptoe. We went to bed late last night. I took them to Itxassou, for the night of the stars. Sacha impressed me, he knows all the constellations.

"It's thanks to your book!" he said.

For Christmas, on Emma's advice, I'd given my nephew a book on astronomy. He'd seemed pleased, but my present couldn't compete with the pair of trainers his parents had left under the tree. I'd been flabbergasted at the size of them:

"My goodness, what shoe size are you?" I'd asked.

"Seven," he'd casually replied.

"But that's not possible! You're ten years old, may I remind you!"

He'd laughed.

"Don't laugh, Sacha! If this goes on, you'll have feet as long as your body, and your classmates will use you to draw their right angles."

"Auntie . . . "

"Having said that, it has its advantages. No need to hire skis, you're already equipped."

He'd rolled his eyes:

"I preferred it when we didn't see you."

I'd been brought down. Everyone had frozen, and the nasty brat had burst out laughing before we could react:

"I'm joking, Auntie! See, I can be funny, too!"

I'd planted a kiss on his head, more than a little proud of my descendant. Emma and Alex had got their breath back, and Alice had come to cling to my neck, as she did to anyone who made a fuss over her brother.

It had been the loveliest Christmas ever. All things had that "last time" intensity to them.

The still-cool air caresses my face. I park my scooter on the sidewalk and go down the steps to the beach. The sun's rays hit the arched rock and gradually reduce the shadows of the build-ings on the sand. In the distance, a woman walks her dog.

Last night, we counted seventeen shooting stars. Alice saw more than that, but we carefully avoided telling her that they were planes. Alex carried her back to car, she'd fallen asleep.

Next week, for the first time, I'll be having Alice and Sacha to stay for the vacation. On my own with them. I've planned far too many activities for one week, but there will be other weeks. So many others. We'll go back to the Rhune, they loved the Pottoks. Sacha wants to learn to surf. Julie will take us out to sea, I hope we'll spot some dolphins.

Although it's impossible to make up for those five lost years, the memories we're making fill the gaps. I love these children madly. On the one hand, because they are hers. Alice has my sister's laugh, Sacha her intense gaze. I see her in them. I ob-serve their relationship, their rapport, the moments only they share, the gentleness of the big brother, the innocence of the little sister, their private language, and I see myself and Emma again, talking together without saying much, falling asleep side by side, holding hands to feel stronger. And on the other hand, because they are themselves. Sacha has a sharp sense of humor and is highly sensitive, he's passionate, his enthusiasm is expansive and his temper volcanic. He reminds me of someone. Alice is loving verging on clingy; she can't bear to be alone, tries her best to be loved, sleeps with a whole flock of soft toys, and steals cookies to gobble up in her room. We find the empty wrappers days later.

They have both become essential to me.

The grains of sand get between my toes. The sand is cool, damp. I put my things down near the water's edge. The tide is going out, hence the darker sand. I walk the few steps between me and the sea. At first, it's always startlingly cold. Then you get used to it.

I considered moving closer to them. Going to live in Alsace, even if it meant leaving my Basque Country and my beloved ocean. Yesterday, once the children were tucked in, Alex announced to me that he'd asked for a transfer.

"Where will you go?" I asked. "I hope it won't be any further away, you're already at the end of the world!"

"Here," he replied. "There's an agency in Bayonne. It's highly sought-after, but with my seniority, I stand a good chance of getting it."

I felt the tears coming.

"That means you'll be coming to live here?"

"Great deduction, Einstein. The children adore you. Although I don't understand why, I can't fight it."

I started to cry and laugh all at once. Not a pretty sight.

"You really are the best of brothers-in-law, Cold Fry!"

He just smiled. That said it all.

The sea is dancing around my hips. I dive in as soon as it's deep enough. I swim level with the shore, holding my breath, wrapped in the silence.

Emma died on February 2.

I was with her. We were with her.

A few days earlier, I'd turned up at the hospital with my laptop and had put *Titanic* on. She'd dozed off several times, exhausted. The closing theme music had woken her up.

"You didn't miss a thing," I'd said. "Jack still dies at the end."

She'd smiled, weakly:

"Jack's death isn't the end of the movie, Gagathe. The end of the movie is Rose taking flight and gorging on life."

I didn't immediately understand. She was passing me a message.

I wish I could say that I don't miss her. I'm learning to live without her, that's all, and not willingly. I still hope to wake up from this nightmare. I'd give everything, absolutely everything, to hear her voice one more time, and not on one of the thousands of videos I took. To nuzzle her neck, concoct a crazy hairstyle for her, come up with a new dance routine, let her tell me I don't sort the knives properly, catch her eye when she's trying not to giggle, anticipate her annoyance when she knows she's late, hear her massacring Céline Dion, see her writing her shopping list alphabetically, and, more than anything, feel her hand in mine. The truth is that I'm haunted by her absence. I search for her in Sacha's eyes, in Alice's smiles, in Alex's every gesture.

I don't yet know how to live without her.

But I'm standing.

Worse, I'm alive.

My sister was right. Jack's death isn't the end of the movie.

There are still plenty of scenes to play out.

I promise you, Emma. I'm going to gorge on life before the closing theme music.

I swim back up to the surface and gulp a great lungful of air.

I can feel it in every cell of my body, like an urge, an instinct, an urgency. Everything's beating faster.

On the horizon, not even a small wave. The ocean is dozing. I tip backwards and stretch out on my back. My hair streams all around me, the sunlight is red behind my eyelids.

Emma loved floating like a log.

I open my hand and can almost hold hers.

THANK YOU

Thanks, Marie, for holding my hand since I was six years old. Apparently, I sulked on the day I heard that our parents were having another baby. You swiftly changed my mind, with your bald head and turds bobbing in the bath. I couldn't have dreamed of a better ally to get through life. Even if we didn't share the same blood, I'd pick you as a sister. I love you, little one.

Thanks to my children, you are my finest inspiration. What a delight to watch you growing up hand in hand, hear you laughing at things only you understand, or arguing and getting over it in a minute, creating shared memories.

Thanks to my husband for being my first reader (a little too zealous, sometimes), allowing my characters to sit at our table, and for sharing my joy at living this totally crazy adventure.

Thanks to my family for your support, your pride, your love. I'm very lucky to have landed among you. Mom, thanks for accompanying me whenever you can—things are better when you're there.

Thanks to my friends for being there at all hours, sharing laughter and tears, and never reproaching me for my silences when writing takes me over.

Thanks to my dearest editor, Pauline Faure. You deny it, but you were invaluable throughout the writing of this book. And big-up Camille for that fakir brush-off!

Thanks to Flammarion, and particularly to Sophie de Closets and Carole Saudejaud, whom I'm happy to find again at this new publishing house, and to Guillaume Robert, Laititia Legay, Marie Nardot, Julie Kowarski, Vincent Le Tacon, François Durkheim, Claire Le Menn, and Sophie Raue for having welcomed me with such warmth and enthusiasm.

Thanks to the Livre de Poche teams: what a joy to continue the adventure with you! A special thank you to Beatrice Duval, Zoé Niedanski, Sylvie Navellou, Anne Bouissy, Ninon Legrand, Florence Mas, Dominque Laude, William Koenig, Bénédicte Beaujouan, Antoinette Bouvier, Maïssoun Abazid, and Céline Selbonne.

Thanks to those early readers of the novel, your feedback was precious to me: Arnold, Muriel, Serena Giuliano, Sophie Rouvier, Cynthia Kafka, Marie Vareille, Baptiste Beaulieu, Camille Anseaume, Alice Morgado, Eva Wenger, and François Coune.

Thanks to the booksellers for being the bridge between readers and authors. And for supporting my books with such zeal.
Thanks to the sales representatives for being the ones who, from the shadows, bring the books out into the light.

Thanks to the bloggers, I'm always moved by the time and energy you spend on sharing your passion.

Thanks to you, dear readers. I've told you before, I'm repeating myself, but this adventure is so wonderful because it's shared with you. Writing was my dream as a little girl; I thought I'd be overjoyed to see my name on a cover. And I am, but I didn't imagine that I'd be most overjoyed by the bond these stories forge with you. Reading your comments is always great, meeting you even greater. Each time I write a new novel, I wonder who it will interest, apart from me. I write about the personal, about feelings I have, situations that move me deeply. I keep saying to myself, as I write: "This isn't going to speak to anyone." I keep going all the same, not letting such thoughts weigh on me. I refuse to be guided by expectations, I want to keep writing with a knot in my stomach and tears in my eyes.

And yet with each novel, you've shown that my apprehension was misplaced. I can't explain it, it's a phenomenon beyond my understanding, but it leaves me thinking that, deep down, we're all a bit the same.

So, thanks for your words, your smiles, your enthusiasm, and your presence. Amidst all this chaos, it's comforting to know that one isn't alone.